LOCKOUT

LOCKOUT

by

Lillian
O'Donnell

G. P. PUTNAM'S SONS
New York

*This is a work of fiction. The events described are
imaginary. The settings and characters are fictitious,
even when the real name of a person or place may be used.
They are not intended to represent specific places or persons,
or, even when the real name of a person or place is used,
to suggest that the events described actually occurred.*

G. P. Putnam's Sons
Publishers Since 1838
200 Madison Avenue
New York, NY 10016

Library of Congress Cataloging-in-Publication Data

O'Donnell, Lillian.
Lockout / by Lillian O'Donnell.
p. cm.
ISBN 0-399-13921-4
1. Mulcahaney, Norah (Fictitious character)—Fiction.
2. Policewomen—New York (N.Y.)—Fiction. I. Title.
PS3565.D59L6   1994   93-42289 CIP
813'.54—dc20

Printed in the United States of America
1   2   3   4   5   6   7   8   9   10

This book is printed on acid-free paper.
∞

LOCKOUT

Chapter 1

"There is no money. As God is my witness, there is no money!"

Magda García pleaded as her son, tire iron in hand, stood in the center of the small stationery store and looked around for something else to smash. He had already raked the shelves and counters clear and the contents were strewn everywhere.

"I swear in the name of the Blessed Virgin Mary, the money's gone."

"Where? What did you do with it?"

"I gave it to you. I gave you everything," she repeated wearily, woefully.

"You lie, old woman." Ricardo García's face was mottled with fury and frustration. "You lie!"

"Ay, Ricardo, it was only a week ago that I gave you what was left. I told you then it was the last. Don't you remember?" his mother asked sadly. "I've given you everything. There is no more."

He wavered, swayed in uncertainty, and for one brief moment Magda García thought she had penetrated his madness. "Here, look." She took a step toward the counter.

He blocked her, his grip on the tire iron tightening. "What are you doing?"

"I just wanted to get my purse to show you the bankbook." Her voice quavered. Since he made no further protest nor offered further threat, she reached around the open end of the counter to the shelf beneath. She opened the shabby handbag and, delving through the jumble of contents, found the passbook. "See? Three thousand five hundred dollars. I took it all out and gave it to you. Last Thursday. Remember?"

CANCELED September 10 was stamped across the final column of figures.

He scowled. Sweat broke out over his sallow skin. "You have other accounts!" he charged. "You've hidden the money in other accounts. Where are they? What banks?"

She was old and frail. He was young and had been a chubby, handsome boy, his parents' pride. The drugs had ravaged him and sapped his strength, yet the desperation of his need made him dangerous.

Sorrow overcame his mother's fear. "*Oh, Ricardo, hijo mío!* What has happened to you? What have you done to yourself?"

"I'm sick, Mama."

"*Sí.* Let me help you." The tears trembled in her eyes.

"Give me the money, Mama."

Slowly, she shook her head. It was no use, she thought.

"I'm in bad trouble, Mama. I need the money."

"We'll go to the police . . . together. I'll come with you. We'll tell them about these bad men, about their threats."

"The police," he sneered. "When have they ever helped?"

Magda García stood before her son, a bent, tired, helpless old woman with stringy hair and raddled cheeks, still mourning the death of her husband of thirty-four years. Unflinching, she looked directly into her son's eyes; then she gestured, indicating the havoc he had wreaked. "This is what's left. This is what we have to depend on for our livelihood," she said, and waited for the fatal blow.

Suddenly he lowered his arm. "I'll be back with my friend," he said. "He'll know how to make you tell where you put the money. I'll be back."

"No you won't."

Luisa García stood a few feet behind her brother. She had been upstairs in the family apartment clearing the breakfast dishes when the destruction began. She'd heard the sounds of splintering furniture and shattering glass. She'd heard her mother's thin pleading. She couldn't make out the words, but their meaning was clear.

Ricky had entered from the street. Luisa had come down the back stairs and let herself in through a private connecting door.

"You're never coming back," she told her brother. "You're never going to beat up on Mama again. You're never going to lay a finger on either one of us, not you and not your buddy." She had the gun in her apron pocket and she pulled it out for her brother to see.

No one moved. Magda García could only stare at her daughter. The brother, crazed by his need, was mesmerized by the gun.

"What do you think you're doing?" he demanded hoarsely. "What the hell do you think you're doing?"

"I told you what would happen if you ever showed your face around here again."

"Luisa, please. *En el nombre de Dios!*" Mrs. García cried out.

"Yeah, Luisa, put the gun down. The damn thing is liable to go off and hurt somebody." Ricardo took a step back.

"I warned you."

"Okay, okay, whatever you want. I'll go away and I won't come back. I'm your brother and I'm in trouble, deep trouble, but if you don't care—"

She fired in the midst of his protestations. She fired three times. All three bullets hit him squarely in the chest. She watched as the blood spurted, saw the surprise on his face, waited till he sank to his knees and keeled over. When she was sure he wouldn't move, she went to the counter, put the gun down, and reached for the wall phone. She dialed 911.

"There's been a shooting. Please send someone right away." In a flat voice she gave her name and address and then hung up. After that, she began to cry, at first quietly, then with racking sobs.

Magda García went to her daughter, put her arms around her and held her, their tears mingling. They were still standing with their arms around each other when the first police patrol car pulled up in front of the store.

Chapter 2

Norah Mulcahaney arrived fifteen minutes before her scheduled appointment. She came up out of the subway directly across the street from the New York Foundling Hospital and wondered what to do with herself. While she hesitated, she automatically catalogued what she saw. The building stood at the corner of Seventeenth Street facing Sixth Avenue. It was plain red brick, the austerity eased by soft aquamarine trim on the ground-floor windows. A cross over the main entrance was the building's only adornment.

Norah crossed over and peered into the lobby. It was smaller than she'd expected, given the size of the building, but equally plain, and it was empty. The public areas of hospitals were usually crowded with doctors, nurses, clerical staff, visitors coming and going. Though she squinted, Norah could see no one.

As soon as she pushed through the plate-glass door, however, before she had a chance to orient herself, a security guard appeared and placed himself in her path.

"What can I do for you?"

"My name is Norah Mulcahaney. I have a nine o'clock

appointment with Sister Beatrice." She didn't show her police ID. She was there as a civilian and didn't want to appear to be pulling rank. "I'm a little early," she explained. "I'll wait." She looked around but couldn't see anything to sit on.

The guard was regarding her with some skepticism.

Why? Did she have a run in her panty hose? Was her slip showing? She had dressed carefully for the meeting, choosing a skirt suit rather than pants, banker's gray with a thin white stripe. Her white silk blouse had a stand-up collar. She never used much makeup—a light dusting of powder, liner to shape her eyes, and a pale lipstick. As one grew older, less was more, Norah thought.

Her hair, a lustrous near black glistening with auburn highlights, was a secret pride. She'd kept it long for many years. At work she would tie it back with colored scarves; off duty she left it loose so that it fell in a soft, dark cloud, contrasting with her white skin and emphasizing the deep blue of her eyes. But now she was forty. Long hair was inappropriate, impractical, out of style. She'd had it cut, finally. It was a wrench, but—she admitted to Monsieur Jacques, the stylist recommended by Officer Webber—she did feel lighter without it, and even younger. Also, the new style minimized the jut of her strong, square jaw, never her best feature. However, neither Monsieur Jacques nor Officer Webber had been able to talk her into touching up the gray—to impress whom? There was no man in her life, nor likely to be.

"Would you sign the visitors' book, please? Ma'am? Ma'am?"

The guard waved her over to a built-in desk along the left wall and handed her a pen. While she signed, he dialed.

"Sister Beatrice? Are you expecting a woman named . . ."

He squinted nearsightedly at the register. "Norah Mulcahaney?" The answer must have been satisfactory, because he bestowed a smile on Norah. "Have a seat." He indicated an alcove screened by a row of potted palms.

"Where? Oh. Yes. I hadn't noticed. Thank you." What was the matter with her? It was all very well to be nervous, but she was sweating and her heart was pounding.

"Lieutenant Mulcahaney?"

She'd barely started for the alcove when a light, musical voice called to her. She turned to see a nun wearing the habit of the Sisters of Charity approaching. Few nuns still wore the traditional garb, and this one was particularly striking and severe. The habit was all black with the narrowest of white collars. The skirt was full, barely skimming the floor and showing only the toes of black leather shoes. A black mantle covered the shoulders. A black bonnet tied under the chin completely covered the nun's hair and hid all but the center of her face.

"I'm Sister Beatrice." She extended her hand.

Norah took it. Though Sister Beatrice appeared slight, her grip was strong.

"Shall we go to my office?"

"All right."

"On the way we can see some of the children."

"Thank you. I'd like that."

The nun led the way to the elevator and they got on.

"As I explained to you on the telephone, the adoption committee meets on an average of once a month," she said. "At that time, persons who have shown an interest in adopting are invited to attend. We describe what kinds of children might be available. Slides are shown and the particular problems of the children are discussed. It's important that prospective parents know the nature of care the children will require and the extent of the commitment, both financial and emotional, they would be making. No paperwork is done until a child becomes available and is matched to a prospective adoptive parent."

"I understand."

"In your situation, since you intend to keep on working . . ."

"I do," Norah put in quickly.

Sister Beatrice nodded. "And because of your past history, I decided it wold be appropriate for us to meet privately."

"I appreciate it, Sister."

The elevator door opened and they stepped out.

"This is the John Coleman School wing," the nun said, leading the way along a narrow corridor.

Norah had a confused impression of one bright, cheery room after another, of infants and toddlers—white, black, Hispanic, Asian—on floor mats playing with young women she assumed to be volunteers, but not playing with each other.

"Paraprofessionals," Sister Beatrice told her. "On a ratio of one for every two children."

Snapshots were tacked on walls, stuffed toys lay everywhere. Row upon row of small, pathetically small, wheelchairs waited in silence for their occupants.

Again Sister Beatrice read Norah's thoughts. "The chairs are built to each child's specifications."

The next thing Norah noticed was the quiet. The usual babble of childish voices was missing. She mentioned it.

"The older children are at school, of course. As for the others . . . it's not always like this. There are days when they scream, hit out, throw things. They are angry children. You'll notice we don't have any mirrors. Too many have been smashed."

They turned a corner and Norah was able to look into

a series of bedrooms. Most had two beds, none more than four. Each was neatly made up, each coverlet different to avoid the institutional look. There were more stuffed animals, at least one to a bed, the private possession of the particular child.

"You take good care of them," Norah remarked. "After what some of them have been through, I'm sure they're happy here."

"Some of them appreciate the food and shelter," Sister Beatrice agreed, "the older ones particularly. But there isn't one that wouldn't give it all up for a mother."

In the maze of snapshots, Norah was drawn to one large framed photograph. It showed a group of adults formally posed.

Sister Beatrice beamed. "Our successes. Our graduates. They came to us as children with various handicaps and were adopted. Supported by the love of good people, they were able to learn to care for themselves and are leading independent and productive lives. We're very proud of them."

"You should be."

"The results are not always so happy," the nun cautioned. "There is no guarantee. But the knowledge that it can and actually has happened is an incentive."

"Sister . . ."

"Here we are." Sister Beatrice opened the door of her office and passed Norah through.

It was no more than a small cubicle, smaller than her own office, Norah thought, and seeming even smaller because of the clutter of snapshots tacked to the walls here as everywhere else. Norah had expected something more impressive and in keeping with Sister Beatrice's title of assistant administrator. The space, she realized, was for the children. She'd also expected Sister Beatrice herself to be of a more commanding presence. Looking beyond the habit, Norah saw a small woman with delicate features. Her pale complexion suggested she didn't get outdoors much.

"Would you like some coffee?" The nun indicated a small side table that held a carafe on a hot plate, and cups.

"Thank you, that would be good. Shall I help myself?"

"Please."

"May I pour you a cup?"

"Thank you. Milk, no sugar, please."

No more was said till the small ceremony was concluded. Each woman continued to size up the other. That was one of the purposes of the meeting, after all, Norah thought, though she was the one who had to pass muster.

Finally Sister Beatrice set her cup aside. "So, Lieutenant Mulcahaney, how many years has it been? I know that we were in the building on Sixty-eighth at the time."

It was evident she'd prepared herself for the interview, Norah thought. That was probably her case file on the desk. "Fourteen years, Sister."

"I was new. I'd just been transferred, but I remember the case. Not a happy outcome."

"For my husband and me—no," Norah agreed. "For Mark, the child, I hope it turned out well."

The nun opened the file folder and leafed through the pages, though she surely knew what was in them. Norah tensed.

"Ah, yes. I'm not permitted to be specific, but I can tell you that the boy was successfully adopted within a short time after you gave him up."

"I'm glad," Norah said, and despite the tears that welled up, she meant it. "It wasn't easy to let him go. We did it, my husband and I, because we believed it was the only way to ensure his safety."

Norah and Joe had wanted a child. After five years of disappointment, they'd decided to adopt. Norah went the route of the agencies. She consulted lawyers and doctors. No luck. Everybody wants a baby, she was told. If she was willing to take an older child, maybe . . .

Her own father had brought Mark, a sturdy toddler, to Norah. At the first sight of him, her heart had melted, but she'd been wary.

"What's wrong with him?"

"Nothing," Patrick Mulcahaney answered.

"Why hasn't someone adopted him?" Norah insisted. "There has to be something wrong."

"All right!" her father snapped. "He's three and a half years old, that's what's wrong with him. The women all want infants. He's too old." Tears of indignation made Pat Mulcahaney's eyes burn.

Even now, so many years later, the memory brought Norah a sharp and painful stab of regret. She could see Mark standing in the middle of her living room, his large brown eyes fixed on her. He hadn't taken her hand when she held it out, but he hadn't turned away either. How many times had he been rejected? Norah wondered, and promised herself to make up for those hurts. But she'd failed. Somehow, Mark's natural mother had found him. She was involved in a case Joe had investigated years back, and she threatened to hurt Mark unless Joe destroyed certain evidence. Even if that had been possible, there was no guarantee that this woman with her organized crime connections wouldn't be back with more demands and more threats.

They'd had no choice but to return Mark.

Norah would never forget the look in the child's eyes when she told him he had to go back. He didn't cry. It would have been easier for both of them if he had. She'd turned him over to Sister Agnes at the day-care center, and he'd walked away without so much as a backward glance. The memory would stay with her forever.

"What assurances can you give me, Lieutenant, that

something like that won't happen again?" Sister Beatrice asked, bringing Norah back to the present.

"It was a very unusual set of circumstances. It's not likely to happen again, but I can't promise it won't."

The nun nodded gravely. "How does Captain Capretto feel about adopting again?"

"My husband died six years ago."

"I'm sorry. I didn't know. You live alone?"

"Yes." She was prepared for the next question and answered without being asked. "I can afford to hire a nanny to take care of the child while I'm at work."

"Do you already know of such a person? The right one may not be so easy to find."

"I intend to take a leave of absence until I do find the right person."

"But you do intend to continue working?"

"Yes. Will that be held against me?"

"A few years back it might have been, but not now. Single parents with the right background and credentials are welcomed. Obviously, as a police officer your credentials are impeccable."

"I'm forty," Norah acknowledged. Might as well get it all on the table.

"Nowadays that isn't considered old."

Norah sighed with relief and was able at last to smile.

"But I'm afraid you're in for a long wait," Sister Beatrice warned. "In that regard, little has changed. There's a huge backlog in the demand for babies. People are traveling to Europe and South America to adopt. Over there the economic situation is so desperate parents are selling one child in order to support the others." Sister Beatrice's face showed her sorrow. She looked hard at Norah.

"I expect to wait. I'll wait as long as I have to."

"Presently, we have twenty-four women in our shelter

for unwed mothers. Most will keep their babies. Those who decide to give them up are few."

"I'll wait."

"There's no guarantee your wait will bring success."

"I understand."

"Would you take a child of Mark's age again?"

"Oh yes."

Sister Beatrice regarded Norah Mulcahaney for a long moment. "The wait would be considerably shorter if you were willing to take on a 'special' child."

Norah sat very straight and squared her shoulders. "You mean mentally or physically handicapped. I've given that a lot of thought. I'm not in a position to take on such a child. I can't make the commitment. I'm sorry, Sister. I wish I could." She stood up. With that answer she'd lost her chance, Norah thought. Settling the strap of her handbag over her shoulder, she prepared to leave.

"Thank you for being honest." Sister Beatrice indicated neither approval nor disapproval. "All right, Lieutenant Mulcahaney, we'll see what we can do."

Norah reached across the desk. This time she was the one who extended her hand.

Chapter 3

It was a beautiful September day: the sun was bright, the air warm, the sky without a cloud. But for Norah Mulcahaney it would have been beautiful even if it had been pouring rain. The interview had gone well, she could feel it; she was positive of it. Leaving the hospital, she turned left to the subway. But she was too excited to go directly to work. It was still early and things were relatively quiet at the Fourth. If anything happened, Ferdi was covering, but even criminals should react benignly on such a day, Norah thought. She decided to get off at the Fifth Avenue station and walk across the park to the West Side. It was a route she took often.

She entered the park at the Arsenal and, heading down into the zoo area, found herself immediately cut off from the clamor of traffic and people on Fifth. The stress of the city seemed to her not to reach in there, nor did the wind. The air was still, almost sultry—heavy with the mellowness of fall. She passed the seal pool and stopped to watch and listen as the Delacorte clock chimed ten and the mechanical animals came out to perform the ritual that never ceased to enchant her. The foliage was already turning and formed a canopy of glowing reds and yellows over the mall. At the Bethesda Fountain, she bought a pretzel from a vendor and sat on a bench overlooking the lake to eat it.

Sister Beatrice liked her and would approve the application, Norah thought. At last there would be a child for her—to hold in her arms and to love. She felt a surge of yearning and allowed herself to imagine what it would be like to have a child in the house again, someone on whom to pour out her love. She permitted herself to dream . . . for a while. A cloud passed over the sun and Norah shivered.

Finishing her snack, Norah crumpled the napkin into a wad and tossed it into the nearest wastebasket. Walking briskly now, she exited the park at Seventy-ninth and reached the Eighty-second Street station house five minutes later. Upstairs in the squad room of the Fourth Homicide Division, Detective Al Sutphin had just put Luisa García into a holding cell.

"What have we got?" Norah asked.

"Woman shot her brother down while the mother watched."

"My God," she whispered.

"Luisa García shot her brother, Ricardo García, while their mother, Magda, watched. Luisa pumped three bullets into her brother and then called nine-one-one for somebody to come and get her."

Baldly put as usual, Norah thought, offering no mitigating circumstances, much less sympathy. He would never change; she should give up hoping. "Why?" she asked, equally laconic.

"The girl says Ricardo was threatening the mother. He wanted money for drugs. She didn't have it, or wouldn't give it to him. Either way, he was going to beat it out of her."

"Beat it out of his mother? Who says?"

"The girl. She told it to the uniforms who responded

to the call, to me, to the assistant M.E., to anybody who asked. She had it down pat. Rehearsed." It was a judgment.

"What does the mother say?"

"I don't know, I haven't gotten around to her yet. I was just going to."

"You brought the mother in?"

"She's a material witness, Lieutenant. Hell, she's an eyewitness. She was there when the murder was committed." Right, Norah thought, again as usual.

When she was assigned the command of the Fourth, Detective First Grade Albert Sutphin had been on the squad three years. She inherited him with the job. Right away she'd sensed he wasn't happy working for her, whether because she was a woman, or because she was younger than he, or hadn't been around as long—any or all of those reasons.

Al Sutphin was a big, shambling man with a dark, saturnine face and light blue eyes that glowed dangerously. He'd had both knees broken in an ambush beating, and that had changed the course of his life. He'd had reconstructive surgery and it was successful. He could walk without pain, but heavy exercise—specifically basketball, which he loved—was out. At the beginning, Sutphin persevered in his rehab routine. Gradually he lost interest. When he saw he couldn't get back to one hundred percent of his previous physical condition, he became morose. He stopped going to the gym for his regular workouts with the therapist. He started to drink. A good investigator, he turned slipshod, and cut corners. It worried Norah. He'd answered her cautious criticism by pointing to his arrest record and his number of cases cleared. It was impressive.

So now Al Sutphin opened his notebook to the appropriate page and read with authority: "Mrs. Magda García runs a small stationery store on Columbus. It was started by her husband, Ramón García, now deceased—cancer of the prostate. They carry the usual items—office supplies, greeting cards, lottery tickets. According to the neighbors, the son, Ricardo, is a crack addict. As long as the father was alive, he kept the kid under some kind of control, but since his death, Ricardo has been running wild. The mother can't do anything with him. He's dropped out of school. All he does is hang out and scheme how to get money for his next fix."

The story was so familiar Norah could have recited it along with Sutphin, but she let him continue.

"He got real deep into debt to his dealer. He went to his mother for the money, begged her for it, told her the dealer would kill him if he didn't pay. Mrs. García gave until she had no more. So then he came back with the dealer and together they trashed the place and took whatever was in the cash register." Sutphin paused briefly. "The girl says they also beat up on the mother."

"She was there?"

"She says she came home from school and found the mother on the floor bloody and bruised. She called nine-one-one and E.M.S. came and took Mrs. García to St. Luke's–Roosevelt for treatment. Then she went out and got herself a gun."

Norah could only shake her head.

"There's more."

Of course, she thought.

"Luisa García went looking for her brother. She warned him to stay away. *She made up her mind*"—Sutphin underscored the words—"that she would never let Ricardo or any of his buddies lay a hand on her mother again."

Everything Sutphin said indicated premeditation. "How do you know she'd made up her mind?" Norah challenged.

Sutphin shrugged. "She told me."

"What about this morning? Was she present when the brother entered the store? Incidentally, I assume it wasn't a break-in, that he had a key?"

"Right. Luisa was in the apartment upstairs and heard the commotion. She knew right away what was happening."

"That's an assumption."

"On her part, not mine, Lieutenant." Sutphin tapped his open notebook. "I put down what she said." Mulcahaney was never satisfied, he thought. As usual, she was trying to punch holes in his case. "When Luisa heard the sounds of furniture being smashed and heard her mother crying, she naturally assumed her brother had come back, so she got her gun and went down to the store," he explained with exaggerated patience.

"And then?"

"Then she shot him three times."

"Just like that? Without a word? Without any kind of warning? Without telling him why?"

"Well, Lieutenant, he knew why."

"And he just stood there and let her do it?"

"What could he do? She was the one with the gun."

"All right. What was he doing when she walked in?"

Sutphin shrugged. "Nothing."

"Was he trashing the place? Threatening his mother?"

"I didn't get into the fine points, Lieutenant," Sutphin retorted testily. "By the time I got there, the whole block had turned out. The street was in an uproar. Both women were in shock. Any further statement was not likely to be reliable. I decided to bring them in."

"You did right."

"Thanks," he replied with a tinge of irony.

Which she ignored. "Did the victim carry a weapon? Did Ricardo García have any kind of weapon on him?"

"We found a tire iron under his body."

"Ah . . ." Maybe there was some hope for the girl after all, Norah thought. "Does Luisa García have a lawyer?"

"I've notified Legal Aid. Someone's on the way."

She didn't need to ask if he'd read the suspect her rights; she'd never known Sutphin to miss, never known him to stumble over a technicality.

"Where've you got her?"

Sutphin led the way to the holding cell and stood to one side so that Norah could get a look at her through the glass before entering.

The girl was sitting at the table in the center, head bowed and resting in her hands. Suddenly she looked up and around as though she sensed she was being observed. She's just a child, Norah thought. Her hair was a mass of tight, dark ringlets, her eyes soft as a doe's, her complexion creamy, flawless. She was beautiful, and a child.

"How old is she?" Norah asked Sutphin. "She can't be sixteen."

"She turned sixteen exactly one month ago."

Norah groaned. An adult. Too old to qualify as a juvenile offender and go before a lenient family court judge. She'd have to bear the full force of an adult trial.

"I'll talk to the mother first," Norah decided. Before entering the interrogation room where Mrs. García waited, Norah looked in to observe her as she had observed her daughter.

The woman sat slumped at the table staring nowhere. It was easy to see where Luisa had gotten her looks, Norah thought. When she was young, Mrs. García must have been exceptionally beautiful. Now her face was raddled; her breasts sagged and her waist was thick. The dark pouches under her eyes were undoubtedly the result of lying awake to listen for her errant son's footfall on the stairs. Her shoulders were permanently rounded

under the weight of mourning for a beloved husband
lost to cancer, and an only son to drugs. Would she now
lose her daughter, too? Norah entered with Sutphin and
introduced herself.

"Sorry to have kept you waiting, Mrs. García."

"Where's my daughter? I want to see my child."

"Of course. We just need you to answer a few questions
first."

"I've already explained what happened. I told this
officer." The grieving woman indicated Sutphin. "And
before him I told the patrol officer."

"I know. Please, be patient," Norah soothed. "Please
go over it once more with me."

"If only Ramón, my husband, were still alive. If only
we'd gone back home to Arecibo and away from the bad
associations like he wanted . . . none of this would have
happened. But we couldn't sell the store, you see. Nobody would buy, no matter what the price, not the way
the neighborhood is now. When we took over the business, it was a fine area—clean, safe, friendly. Now, nobody walks alone to the corner. We go in pairs to the
market. We don't go out after dark. Our money was all
tied up in the store, so when we couldn't sell it, we
couldn't go.

"Business was bad. We opened early and closed late,
as late as we dared. My husband was undergoing chemo-
therapy. It was too much for him. Once Ramón was
gone, Ricardo went out of control. He moved to a place
of his own, but he came to me when he needed money.
I gave him what I could, but it was never enough. Then
one night he came with his dealer. He was a man, not
a teenager, a big man, and he hit me so hard he broke
my jaw. Ricardo watched."

And that had hurt more than the blow, Norah
thought. "Did you report this to the precinct?"

"Yes, yes, I did. But they couldn't do anything."

"What do you mean, they couldn't do anything?"

"They said Ricardo had an alibi and so did the dealer. They were both somewhere else when it happened. Their friends swore it. The police believed they were lying, but there was no way to prove that. They said no matter how many complaints I made, his friends would swear he was somewhere else. They advised me to get an order of protection. Then they told me I would have to serve it myself." Her voice broke. "How could I do that?"

They could have gotten Ricardo García as he was making a buy, or raided his place and gotten him on possession, Norah thought. If he had been up in the drug hierarchy they might have, but he wasn't important enough for their time. Everybody was spread too thin. That left people like Luisa and her mother to protect themselves in any way they could.

"Let's talk about this morning, Mrs. García. When Ricardo came to the store, was he alone?"

"Yes."

"And he had a key?"

"Yes, but I was already there."

"So he just walked in. Then what happened?"

"He wanted money. I told him I didn't have it. He went crazy. He started smashing things."

"What did he use to do this?"

"He had a bar, an iron bar."

"What did he destroy?"

Magda García sighed. "The copying machine, the fax, a display case . . ."

"Did he threaten you with the bar?"

Mrs. García hesitated.

"Did he say, 'I'll hit you if you don't give me money'? Did he raise the iron bar against you?"

Al Sutphin scowled. The lieut' was leading the witness, putting words into her mouth. It was not proper. She ought to know better. She did know better.

Magda García considered. She didn't want to admit that her son had been ready to beat her with an iron bar, but he was dead and her daughter was alive and at risk. She understood that this woman police officer was trying to help her. "Yes, he did threaten me with it. If Luisa hadn't shot him when she did, he would have brought it down on me."

"All right, Mrs. García, that's all for now. You're free to go."

"My daughter, you said I could see my daughter. You promised."

"Of course, but it will be a while. Why don't you go home and her lawyer will contact you."

"Lawyer?"

"From Legal Aid, Mrs. García. There'll be no charge."

"He can't be very good if he works for nothing."

"If you want to hire somebody else, that's your decision, Mrs. García."

"I don't have any money."

Norah cast a glance at Sutphin. "Go home, Mrs. García. Get some rest."

The woman shook her head. "I'll wait. Is there somewhere I can wait?"

"Downstairs."

They walked her from the interrogation room to the elevator. When the doors had closed on her, Al Sutphin turned to his boss.

"What are you looking for, Lieutenant? It's open-and-shut. The girl's confessed. She admits buying the gun for the specific purpose of killing her brother. No matter what the mother says, you can't get around that." He was right, Norah knew, but she wasn't ready to admit it.

Chapter 4

Tuesday, September 22
11:00 p.m.

After fourteen straight hours of rehearsal, Bo Russell called it off.

Weary, tempers frayed, singers, musicians, and technicians wasted no time getting out. Only Bo stayed behind. Alone in the empty, silent studio, he began to pick out the last eight bars of the new song, the song that was to be the signature number of the album, "Stop Stompin' on My Heart," on the electronic keyboard. He listened each time as the last reverberations were absorbed by the baffles his own engineer had set up around the room. It just wasn't right. It didn't work. Triumph's Studio A was the largest and considered the finest recording facility in New York. It was sought after by both classical and pop artists. Toscanini had conducted there. Barbra Streisand had cut the record that made her a star there. Bo Russell had hoped that somehow the inspiration would be passed on to him.

He tried variations of the final chords. Didn't help. He went back and started over from the top. The music carried his anguish, swelled with it, then at the end finished with a wail when it should have exploded.

The call for the next session was eleven tomorrow morning. He had to get it right by then. He'd already spent too much money on studio time. Early in his career, Bo Russell had been able to improvise during the actual recording. In those days the excitement and tension of the process fed his creativity. He'd lost that; success had robbed him of it. Success had burdened him with too many responsibilities. He had held his position at the top of the chart for three years and then, for no reason he could figure, had started to slide—no, fall. He was, in fact, in a free-fall right now. The fans just weren't buying. He needed another hit, needed it badly. And sitting here wasn't doing any good. He should take a break too. He got up, crossed to the plain wooden door. Fishing in his pocket, he found the key and locked the door behind him. He turned the corner to the lounge area.

"Ellie!"

Curled up on one of the facing sofas in a small area used by the artists for relaxing between sets was the woman who had discovered Bo Russell and guided him up the ladder—his agent, Eleanor Lyras. She slept, face buried in a pillow.

"Ellie?" Bo bent over and shook her gently by the shoulder.

She opened her light gray eyes and smiled up at her top client, her biggest money-maker. She was genuinely fond of him.

"How long have you been out here?" he asked.

She checked the clock on the wall. "A couple of hours."

"You should have let me know."

"I didn't want to interrupt the rehearsal."

"Believe me, an interruption would have been welcome," Bo said wryly. "I just can't get the handle on the number, Ellie. I don't know what's wrong. I've heard of writer's block, but I always thought it was an excuse for laziness. I never thought it could happen to me."

"You haven't got a block," she soothed in her soft, low voice. "Your problem is that you're trying for perfection."

"I'm a long way from it, believe me." He went over to the coffee machine.

Eleanor Lyras swung her long, slim legs over the side, unfolded her lanky body, and straightened to her full six-foot height. There was a cool and composed air about her which her Nordic coloring—pale skin, long silver-blond hair, held in place by a headband—emphasized. No one who knew Lyras had ever seen her out of control. She was only five years older than Bo Russell, but she treated him with the indulgence of a doting aunt.

He filled a couple of mugs with coffee, handed her one, and sat down opposite her.

"So? What's up?" he asked. His round face and blond hair, cut in a blunt line at the earlobes, gave him a naive, country-boy look.

"Money," she replied promptly. "It's going out, but it's not coming in. We've got to cut expenses."

"I know record sales are slow, but we're not in any real trouble, are we?"

"Depends on what you call trouble. We owe everybody. We leave a trail of debt wherever we go." She paused. "We're going to have to cancel the Meadowlands. We were counting on advance ticket sales to meet the guarantee, but there's no demand, none."

He took it well. "I always said that place was too big for us. It doesn't suit our style. We need something more intimate. Like the Paramount, for instance. Get us a date there."

"They say they're booked solid."

"Even the Garden would be acceptable. It's not all that big."

Lyras shook her head. "They're solid too."

That pierced his defense. His young-looking face sagged into one older than his years. "They don't want me."

"When 'Stop Stompin' on My Heart' hits the stores, they'll want you, believe me."

"Sure."

"They will, Bo, I promise."

He was still worried. "How about Shea for October second? Is that still on?"

"Absolutely." She reached over and patted his hand. "But in the meantime, we've got to do some damage control."

"Like what?"

"To start with, there's Ben. I think he's got his hand in the till."

"No way. He's my brother. I give him whatever he wants—all he has to do is ask. Why should he steal?"

"You can't give him what you haven't got, so he takes whatever he can get his hands on. I think he's skimming the box office receipts."

Bo Russell shook his head decisively. "No."

"If you won't take him out of the box office, at least warn Herb to keep an eye on him. I'll speak to Herb, if you want."

Bo shook his head again. "I'll do it."

"And Gloria's got to put a brake on the shopping," the agent continued. "The bills she's running up! My God, she's another Imelda Marcos."

"Come on, Ellie. I know you don't like her, but that's not fair."

Nobody liked her, Ellie thought. "It's got nothing to do with liking her," she said.

"Nobody tries to see her side of it." Bo Russell defended his wife. "She's trying her best to fit in. Why can't you give her a chance?"

No use talking to him, Lyras thought. After five years he still didn't get it. What would it take to open his eyes?

The truth was that despite her constant complaints to Bo, Gloria Russell was well satisfied with her condition. She enjoyed all the benefits of the artistic life without any of the burdens. She traveled with the group, stayed in the best hotels, ate in the finest restaurants, wore fancy clothes. She neither cooked nor did a lick of housework and bore none of the stress of performing. There was plenty of anxiety in the music business. For all the glamour of their life, the big bucks didn't come easy to pop artists. Take Bo as an example. It was routine for the solo artist and lead singer of The Earth Shakers—a sensation since his win four years ago of the New York Music Award for the best male rock artist—to leave his dressing room just before showtime and step out into the alley to throw up. That done, he went back to check his makeup and made his entrance to the wild acclaim of his fans. He performed, and when he came off he was drenched in sweat and trembling, having lost anywhere from ten to fifteen pounds.

The recording sessions weren't easy either; they put a different kind of strain on him. Lately the sessions were running longer and longer because, as Lyras said, he was growing more demanding of himself, of his backup singers, the band, the crew. Everybody had come to dread the playbacks because Bo was never satisfied. What in the past had been a three-hour session consisting of two or three takes could last twenty hours. Studio time didn't come cheap. But it wasn't only a matter of expense; the nervous strain was transmitted to everybody. Bo was even getting into editing and had hired his own engineer to supervise the mix.

Gloria Russell, however, was not subject to rehearsals

that lasted all night and sometimes into the morning. Gloria seldom if ever attended rehearsals. She appeared at the concerts or at a session when there was a reasonable expectation that it would result in a final take. Then she arrived, dressed to the hilt, to hold court. She was thirty-five, a hard-lived thirty-five, the oldest of the wives or girlfriends on the tour. Collagen injections plumped up the lines in her face. Her rock star makeup—a heavy white foundation, black liner to outline her eyes, heavy mascara, scarlet lips, and spiky platinum hair—drew attention away from what the injections couldn't eliminate.

"So she goes on a shopping spree every now and then," Bo went on. "What else does she have to do? I'm either performing or rehearsing. I have no time to spend with her. She's lonely, so she goes shopping and runs up a few bills. If I can't provide some pleasure for my wife, what the hell am I in this business for?"

"I don't know," Ellie Lyras replied meekly, surprised at the outburst.

"Anything else?" he demanded. "Can we afford the studio?" he asked sarcastically.

"Actually . . ." Lyras hesitated. "Do we really need the studio on lockout?"

"Yes!" he thundered.

Their eyes met and held. Bo backed down first. "I'm sorry, Ellie. You're right about everything. You always are. I'll speak to Gloria about cutting down."

Much good that would do, the agent thought, but said no more.

"I do need to have access to the studio, though. Just give me a couple more days. I know I can work it out."

"Sure you can. You're a big talent, Bo. I knew that from the first time I heard you sing with your church choir. A shiver went through me then. It still does every time I hear you, no matter where. We've come a long way together. We've got a long way still to go."

*   *   *

It was a balmy night and the Park West wasn't far from the studio, which was one of the reasons he stayed there, so Bo decided to walk. He picked up his key at the desk and went straight upstairs and let himself in. A single lamp was lit in the sitting room. Both bedrooms were dark. Gloria and he used separate rooms because of his erratic schedule; it wasn't fair to disturb her sleep with his comings and goings. Walking quietly, he went over to her room. The door was ajar; he pushed it a little farther so he could look inside. By the spill of light, he could see the bed was empty. He scowled. It was still early, of course. Probably she'd gone to a movie. He couldn't expect her to sit in the room alone. Still, he wished that on this particular night she'd been there. He reached for the wall switch, turned on the lights, and stepped inside. How long was it since he'd been in her room? How long since he'd been in her bed? He looked around like a stranger.

The room was redolent of her, heady with the scent of her body melding with that of Joy, one of the most expensive perfumes in the world. He went over to her vanity table cluttered with jars, bottles, a palette of rainbow eye colors, all the artifices she used. She didn't need them, Bo thought. He loved her as she was, not what she was trying to make herself into.

Next he looked in her closet. There were clothes there he'd never seen, clothes he was sure she'd never worn. Ellie was right, Gloria was spending a lot of money. She seemed to have a compulsion to buy, to possess. Once a thing was hers, she no longer had any interest in it. He touched the clothes, felt the silks and satins and soft brushed suedes. He fingered the beaded and sequined gowns and imagined her wearing them.

With a sigh, Bo Russell turned out the lights and left his wife's room and crossed the sitting room to his. Guiding himself only by the illumination from the street, he pulled a chair up to the picture window that overlooked the park. He had no idea how long he sat like that, perhaps he dozed, but the sky was still dark when he awakened with a sudden start. He got up, turned on the nearest lamp, and reached for the telephone. He dialed his manager's room.

"Herb? I want everybody in the studio by . . ." He checked his watch. "Make it five. That gives them plenty of time."

Wednesday, September 23
3:45 a.m.

Herb Cranston groaned and looked at the bedside clock. Damn. No use mentioning the hour to Bo—he didn't care. He felt like recording and that's all that mattered to him. That was why he rented the studio on lockout, an expensive arrangement which ensured that nobody besides himself and The Earth Shakers could use the facility during a specified period. Members of the group could leave their property—instruments or personal effects—with the assurance they would be safe. Most important, Bo could get in to work whenever the spirit moved him, as apparently it did now. On such occasions, it was Herb Cranston's job to get hold of and assemble everybody to await Bo's arrival.

Like many of the group, Cranston came from Bethlehem, Pennsylvania, Bo's hometown. Like them, he had worked for the mill, the town's principal employer. Studying at night, he had crossed over from blue collar to white collar and was working in the account-

ing office when Bo offered him the job as his business
manager. It raised Cranston to a level he had never even
dreamed about. Inevitably, there had to be inconveni-
ences. Yawning, he sat up and turned on the bedside
light.

In the drawer of the nightstand, Cranston kept a list
of the singers, musicians, and engineers with their cor-
responding room numbers. One of the advantages of
their staying at the same hotel was that they were all
within easy reach. Propped up in bed, the manager lit
a cigarette and started dialing.

They straggled into Studio A singly and in groups.
Grumbling at having been summoned out of warm beds
before dawn, they consoled themselves with containers
of hot coffee and pastries and kept the complaints to
themselves.

The star sat at the electronic keyboard in the center
of the big, bare room, blond head bowed as he fingered
the keys lightly. When he raised his head and looked
around, that was the signal for everybody to stop the
chatter and come to attention. As lead singer, artist, and
star, Bo was the one responsible for the success of The
Earth Shakers. He carried the group on the strength of
his talent, and was responsible for the fast ride to the
top of the charts. He looked around again and fixed
finally on his backup singers. There were three where
there should have been four.

"Where's Ben?"

No answer.

Bo directed himself to his manager. "Where's Ben?
Did you get hold of him?"

"He was the first one I called," Cranston replied. "He
said he'd be right over."

Bo looked at the clock on the wall over the control

room. The hands pointed to five precisely. "We'll wait. Ten minutes."

The tension translated into movement and talk, more coffee and pastry, more cigarettes lit and ground out. As the minute hand of the clock swept to the new deadline, activity died down and everyone watched Bo.

"Who can we get to fill in?" Bo asked. "We need somebody to get here fast."

It was not an unusual situation, or an unusual solution. Nobody considered Bo Russell was dumping his brother. The arrangement they were about to record called for four voices in the backup, and four voices were essential. Time was money. It was simply a matter of not being able to wait.

A backup singer, Andy Link, spoke up. "What about Mel Deever? He's in town."

Bo nodded. "Get him."

That meant more waiting. Eyes shifted from Bo to the clock to the door. Would Ben show up before his replacement? Whether before or after, what would Bo's reaction be? He was known to be tolerant of his brother's behavior as long as it didn't affect the performance. Bo was fiercely dedicated to his music and demanded a like commitment from everybody else. Holding up the session was not something he could disregard. But it was Deever who showed up first, so the confrontation was postponed.

Where the hell was Ben? Everybody wondered, but nobody really cared as they got down to work. By seven a.m. they were ready to lay down tracks. "Okay, let's do it," Bo said. He took off the earphones and strode to the isolation booth in the far corner of the room. He opened the door.

And stood there.

His back was to the rest of the room. No one could

see his face or guess why he remained transfixed. After several moments, he went down on his right knee and reached out a hand.

"Ben?" he murmured. "Ben . . .?"

Herb Cranston went over and looked over Bo's shoulder.

"Somebody call the cops."

Chapter 5

Wednesday, September 23
7:16 a.m.

Everybody moved fast on this one. The first officers to reach the scene marked it top priority and notified the detectives at the Two-oh. They passed it on to the Fourth Division Homicide located overhead. Sergeant Fernando Arenas caught the squeal and immediately notified his superior, Lieutenant Norah Mulcahaney, at her home. She jumped into the gray pants and jacket she kept as her standard outfit for just such occasions, when she had no idea what conditions would be and no time to fuss over what to wear. She was dressed and at the scene before eight.

Phillip Worgan, Chief Medical Examiner of the City of New York, came himself. Six feet tall and heavy, his weight was disguised by the loose tweeds he always wore. He had a swarthy complexion, bushy brows, and a long, narrow nose—one of those men who were homely and yet attractive. The attraction came from his enthusiasm, Norah thought. She didn't know many more zealous in their work than Phil Worgan.

The two met at the street entrance of Triumph Studios and climbed the single flight up to Studio A together.

Never having been in a recording studio before, Norah looked around curiously. It was just a big bare room. Large rectangles of what looked to her like cardboard placards were set up along the walls. She had seen them in concert halls; they were called baffles, and were used to control the acoustics. An electronic keyboard was set in the center of the studio, a microphone on a stand positioned between it and the bench. The musicians, holding tight to their instruments, were bunched against the wall at the far end.

A motley crew, Norah thought. The uniform seemed to be flannel shirts and torn jeans. There were a few in leather and metal, but apparently both styles were passé. Grunge was in, she'd read somewhere, and now that she saw it she had no trouble recognizing it: baggy pants, rock T-shirts, weather-worn leather jackets—all bought in thrift shops. The style was in mixing and matching with velvet and lace and chains and baker boy caps, and layering was key. The principal component was the hair—lank and greasy. They were young, in their early twenties, and subdued—uncharacteristically so, she assumed. Despite the rampant violence of the times, Norah guessed they had not stood in the presence of sudden death before.

A booth about the size of a pair of old-fashioned telephone kiosks, at the opposite end of the studio, was the focus of police attention. It was paneled halfway up to waist height and the upper portion was glass. The crime scene detectives were dusting for prints; the photographers were setting up their shots. Seeing Worgan and Mulcahaney, they stepped aside.

The victim was in the booth sitting on the floor, knees bent, tucked nearly to his chin in order to fit into the space. He couldn't have fallen into that position, Norah thought. To get a look at him, Norah had to get down on her knees and peer up into his face. He was flushed, bloated. His brown eyes were wide open and bloodshot. His jowls were heavy. The tan gabardine, western-style outfit he wore was too tight for him. The shirt buttons strained against the fabric and the silver buckle of the rawhide belt cut into the soft flesh of his bulging belly. But what mattered to Norah and Worgan was the blossom of blood that matted his chest hair and had soaked into the material of the shirt.

Sergeant Ferdi Arenas came over. "Morning, Lieutenant. Morning, Doctor."

Ferdi Arenas and Norah Mulcahaney went back a long way together, all the way to her first command. They had supported each other through personal and professional crises. When Ferdi's fiancée, Pilar Nieves, a policewoman working as a decoy, had been killed in front of him, he had come close to quitting the force. Norah had persuaded him to stay. It had taken him five years to start dating again. Now he was married and the proud father of twin girls and a baby boy.

Ferdi was ten years younger than Norah. He was of medium height and slim. The joy of his marriage had filled out his slight frame and eased the deep furrows across his brow and put bounce in his step. But the premature gray in his dark hair was spreading. He had recently started to cultivate a pencil-thin mustache.

As for Norah, after her husband, Joe Capretto, was shot down by muggers, she had remained alone for almost as long as Ferdi. Then she'd met Randall Tye, a celebrated newsman. They were mutually attracted, but at first Norah resisted. She didn't know why. A precognition of disaster? She managed to convince herself to set it aside, when tragedy struck again. Randall was murdered. Losing Joe had cut Norah's life in two: her work and her loneliness. When she came home and put the key in the lock, she opened the door to silence. All these years later, it hadn't changed—till Randall. He filled the void; he brought her laughter. Then silence claimed her again.

"What've you got?" Norah asked.

"The victim is Ben Russell, Bo Russell's brother." Arenas paused. Ben wasn't famous, but Bo had exploded on the folk-rock-gospel horizon a scant five years ago. Whether you were into pop music or not, you'd heard about him. Norah was not, but looking over the group of performers, she could pick him out. That wasn't only because she had seen his picture so many times, but because he'd set himself apart, placing a chair so that he could keep an eye on the open door of the booth. The brothers didn't resemble each other, Norah thought, looking from one to the other. Bo was younger and physically fit. But at this moment he was gray with shock and fatigue. His round face glistened with sweat. He watched every move of the detectives working around his brother's form, flinching every time they came close to touching him.

"Bo found him," Ferdi told Norah. "A recording session had been scheduled for five a.m., but Ben didn't show."

"Five a.m.?" Norah repeated.

"Right. It wasn't unusual. The studio was rented on what they call lockout, meaning the renter has exclusive rights to its use for an agreed period and everybody else is locked out. Bo was in the habit of working whenever the spirit seized him, and this morning at three forty-five he felt creative. He contacted his manager and instructed him to get everybody over here by five. Everybody showed up but Ben."

Who was already here, Norah thought. "Nobody looked inside the booth?"

"There was no reason."

"So they sat around and waited?"

"For ten minutes. Then they got a replacement."

"Ah . . ."

"Studio time is expensive. It can run up to two hundred fifty an hour."

"So the victim was in this . . ."

"Isolation booth," Ferdi prompted. "They use it to separate the lead singer from the backup and the instrumental so that if they get a satisfactory track on one and the other's no good, they don't have to throw everything out."

"So the victim had to be in the booth by five this morning when the rehearsal started," Norah reasoned.

"Earlier," Arenas said. "They started straggling in at about four-thirty."

"And if Bo hadn't decided to use the isolation booth when he did, Ben might still be lying there," she concluded, and moved closer for another look.

The way he was positioned—head down, chin resting on his chest, eyes open—made him appear to be staring at his wound in surprise, Norah thought.

Worgan had listened to Ferdi Arenas's remarks with interest. The physical evidence should be consistent with the medical. He got down on one knee for his examination. It was brief but thorough. "I'd say the killer stood outside the booth and fired through the open door. He fired twice, both shots close to the heart. The gun was probably a twenty-two and the victim was a big man."

"And he just stood there and took it?" Norah asked, the same question she had asked with regard to the García shooting.

"You think two people could squeeze into that space and there would be room for one to pull a gun on the other?" Worgan retorted. "Where are the powder marks?"

Norah frowned. "He was killed in the studio and then placed in the booth?"

"All right. That's possible," Worgan allowed.

"What about time of death?"

"If, according to the sergeant"—Worgan acknowledged Ferdi—"people started straggling in at about four-thirty, it had to be over by then. Rigor hasn't set in. There are no traces of lividity. We'll have to check temperature and stomach contents. You know how it goes."

"Okay." Norah nodded. "That's it for me."

Worgan signaled to the attendants to prepare the body for transport. As they unfolded the body bag, Bo Russell jumped to his feet.

"What are you doing?"

"Mr. Russell?" Norah blocked his way. "I'm Lieutenant Mulcahaney. This is Dr. Worgan and Sergeant Arenas. We're very sorry for your loss."

"Are you in charge?"

"Yes."

"What are you doing with my brother?" Bo Russell's face was drawn. Lines that had lurked beneath the surface appeared suddenly like sharp, deep cuts, and the sweat gathered in them. "Where are you taking him?"

"To the morgue."

He flinched.

"I'm sorry. There has to be an autopsy."

"Why? Isn't it obvious he was shot?"

"Police procedure," Norah replied quietly.

Russell shook his head but made no further protest. Stoically, he watched as his brother was placed in the bag and the zipper closed. In that moment, for Bo, his brother passed from life to death. He continued to watch as the sack was lifted to the gurney and securely strapped and wheeled out of the studio. By then, it was bereft of humanity.

Gently, Norah broke into his reverie. "I don't like to intrude on your grief, Mr. Russell, but there a few questions I need to ask. Is there somewhere we can talk?"

"The lounge. This way."

At Norah's indication, Ferdi went with them.

Russell led the way to the same alcove where a few hours ago he and Ellie Lyras had talked. The large coffee urn had been replenished and there was a fresh supply of pastry. He indicated the spread. "Help yourselves, please." He sat.

Both declined. Norah sat opposite the singer; Ferdi remained standing.

"When was the last time you saw your brother, Mr. Russell?" Norah asked.

He answered promptly. "Last night when we broke."

"That was . . .?"

"Eleven."

"Everybody left? Including Ben?"

"That's right."

"What about you?"

"I stayed for a while, tried to work, couldn't. So I went back to the hotel."

"What time was that?"

"I don't know." Suddenly a thought occurred to him. "Ask Ellie, Ellie Lyras, my agent. She was waiting for me right here in this lounge. We had a talk and then went our separate ways."

"What did you talk about?"

For a moment, Norah thought he'd refuse to answer. Then he shrugged. "Business. Ticket sales, bookings, things like that."

"This meeting with your agent, was it scheduled?"

"No. We were supposed to work right through. Ellie came as she always does to give support, to be available . . . just in case."

"But the session didn't go well, so you broke off. You stayed behind and worked alone for a while, then gave up. On the way out you found Miss Lyras, talked to her, then went back to your hotel—alone. Is that it?"

"Yes."

"Who locked up? I assume somebody did; there were expensive instruments left behind."

"I locked up. I have a key."

"Who else has one?"

"Herb Cranston, my manager."

"And somebody from the studio, naturally."

"Naturally."

"When was the next session scheduled?" She was asking the easy questions first, the questions that elicited almost automatic replies.

"Eleven this morning."

"But at three forty-five you changed your mind and called everybody back. Why?"

"I went back to the hotel, but I didn't go to bed—I was too charged up. I was having trouble with one of the numbers. Actually, it's the album's signature number. I kept going over it in my head. I sat. I got up. I paced. I sat again. I suppose I dozed. All I know is that all of a sudden I had it—the solution. I was excited. I couldn't wait to get it on tape."

"I guess the creative process can't be restricted between nine and five," Norah observed. "All this pacing in the middle of the night must be hard on your wife. She *is* on this trip with you? It seems to me I read somewhere . . ."

For the first time Bo Russell smiled. His face softened. "We have separate rooms, Lieutenant. If we didn't, poor Gloria would never get any sleep."

"So she has no idea what time you got in or what time you went out?"

"No, she doesn't."

"After instructing your manager to call your people, you got dressed and came back here. Were you the first to arrive? Of course, you had to be: no one else had a key." Then she added, "Except for Mr. Cranston."

"My mix engineer, Duggie Watts, and a backup singer, Rollo Dubois, were waiting on the street out front. We came in together."

"What time was that?"

"I have no idea," he snapped. "I wasn't clocking myself. I didn't know I'd be required to account for every minute of my time."

"Sorry," Norah apologized. "I'm sure Mr. Watts or Mr. Dubois will remember. Sergeant." She turned to Ferdi. "Will you ak Mr. Cranston to come in?" She got up and went over to the refreshment table. "I think I will have some coffee, after all. How about you, Mr. Russell? May I pour you a cup?"

He took a deep breath. "All right. Yes."

"This must be a terrible shock for you," Norah said, handing him a cup.

"It is."

"Were you and your brother close?"

"Oh yes. Our parents died when I was eight and Ben was fourteen. Our only relative was an aunt. She had three kids of her own and she couldn't afford to take two more. Social Services tried to split us up. We ran away. Ben looked old for his age, so he got a job and he supported us. He kept us together. He didn't finish school himself, but he saw to it that I did. He encouraged me in my singing. I didn't have much confidence—he had it for me. He found out Ellie Lyras was in town looking for talent and he contacted her and got her to come and listen to me. If it hadn't been for Ben, I'd still be working in the mill."

There was a light tap at the door and Ferdi ushered

in Herbert Cranston. The manager was a stolid six foot two—a contrast to the thin, sallow musicians. His head was large and his features were bold, appropriate to his frame. He wore a conservative three-piece suit of gray flannel. His long brown hair was pulled back and secured by a rubber band. Straddling the cultures, Norah thought.

"Coffee, Mr. Cranston?"

He hadn't expected the informality. A quick look at his boss, who held a cup, reassured Cranston. "Thanks. I'll help myself."

Norah waited till he had done so and had sat down. "There are some gaps in Mr. Russell's recollection of events from last night into this morning. Perhaps you can fill them for us."

Cranston moved forward to the edge of the seat, fully attentive.

"Last night's session broke at eleven. I assume you were here."

"Oh yes."

"Good. What did you do after?"

"I went directly back to the hotel, the Park West."

"Alone?"

"Yes. I had work to do. Anyway, I don't fraternize much. In my job, that's not a good idea."

"I see. All right, you went back to your room and worked. Then what?"

"I went to bed about one."

"And then?"

"Bo called. It was three forty-five. I checked the clock automatically as soon as the phone rang."

"So his calling you at such an hour was not unusual?"

"By no means."

"And he wanted you to get everybody together to go back to work by five. Surely that was short notice?"

"Again, not really. It gave us a little more than an

hour. When we're on the road like this, we mostly all stay at the same hotel, one that's also close to the studio or arena. I have a list of the room numbers. That's all there is to it."

"Did you contact Ben Russell?"

"Of course. He was the first one."

"Why was that?"

"He's Bo's brother." Cranston shrugged, indicating that should be obvious.

"He was in his room? He answered his phone? You spoke to him and he was all right? This was at . . .?"

"Immediately after Bo hung up."

"Had Ben been sleeping? Could you tell?"

"He sounded like he might have been."

"Was he annoyed at being awakened at such an hour?"

"Sure he was annoyed, but he was used to it like everybody else. It's part of the job."

"And he said he'd be here?"

"Naturally."

"So when he didn't show up, you must have been surprised. What did you think had happened?"

"I had no idea. I couldn't imagine."

Norah switched to Bo Russell. "What did you think had happened, Mr. Russell? Did your brother have a tendency to be late?"

The manager answered for him. "He did not. Time is money in this business, Lieutenant. We can't afford that kind of self-indulgence from a star, much less a backup singer. He would have found himself permanently replaced."

"Didn't it occur to either one of you to call his room again? Just in case he'd decided to catch a couple more winks and had fallen asleep again?"

Both star and manager shook their heads.

"You're sure it was Ben you spoke to?"

"Of course I'm sure," Cranston replied.

"No chance you were mistaken?"

"Who else could it have been? I know Ben's voice. Who else would be answering his phone?" Cranston scowled. "Do you think I'm trying to provide myself with an alibi? Is that what this is about? I don't need an alibi. I had nothing to do with Ben's death."

"Do you think he's lying to help *me*?" Bo Russell asked. "I didn't kill my brother, Lieutenant."

"Then you won't mind being searched," Norah concluded. "Your brother was shot with a low-caliber weapon, probably a twenty-two, easy to conceal."

Russell spread out both arms. "Go ahead."

Norah nodded to Arenas. Quickly and expertly, he patted the singer down.

"He's clean."

"Mr. Cranston? Any objection?"

"None."

Same procedure, same result.

"Have you any idea why your brother was killed?" Norah asked the star.

"None."

"Mr. Cranston?"

The manager shook his head.

"We'd like to search everybody," Norah told Russell. "It would help if you'd tell them to cooperate."

"I can't order them."

"Has it occurred to you, Mr. Russell, that your brother's killer might be in the building? That he might still have the murder weapon on him?"

"I'll ask them," he said.

Chapter 6

Rollo Dubois, backup singer, and Duggie Watts, engineer and his roomie, readily confirmed what Bo Russell had told Norah—that they were waiting in the street in front of Triumph Studios when Bo arrived to unlock the door. Then the three of them entered together and went up the stairs to the second floor and Studio A. They weren't exactly sure about the time, but thought it was between 4:30 and 4:45. They agreed with Bo Russell's account of the events that led to his opening the door of the isolation booth and finding the body of his brother inside.

Watts was short with a massive, well-developed upper body and bandy legs. He was starting to go bald, but Norah didn't think he was much older than thirty. He wore chinos and a dark shirt open at the throat. Like Cranston, he was making a statement by what he wore, setting himself apart. By contrast, his roomie, Rollo, was the picture of the conception of the typical rock musician. He was thin and pale, with a cascade of crimped brown curls that fell to his shoulders. Sartorially, he was into grunge. Physically different though they were, their eagerness to support each other and the looks they exchanged indicated a strong bond.

The story was repeated by each person present with almost no variation. No one objected to being searched. The sense of loyalty to Bo was very strong. Norah was impressed.

She was not surprised that the gun didn't turn up. The perp would have been crazy not to get rid of it. Ascertaining that the group would remain in Manhattan at least until October 2, when they were booked into Shea, Norah released everyone. Ferdi called the squad for help in a thorough toss of the whole building. Wyler, Neel, and Ochs, along with four uniforms, responded.

After two hours they came up empty and called it off. It was logical to assume the perp left the building, taking the gun with him. How he got out was no big problem. How he'd gotten in was. Even more puzzling was how to account for Ben Russell's presence. At this point, Norah couldn't even guess.

Wednesday, September 23
2:00 p.m.

The station house was oddly quiet.

"Where is everybody?" Norah asked the desk sergeant.

"Down at City Hall for the big rally. Don't you remember, Lieutenant?" Ed Brownsteen replied.

"Oh, sure, but I thought—" Norah stopped. The P.B.A. had called the rally to protest formation of a new, all-civilian board to review complaints against police. Only off-duty cops were entitled to attend. Realistically, it was expected that some on-duty cops would find their way down there. The empty halls and the silence at the

Two-oh suggested that a number of the men and women of that precinct had already done so.

Norah frowned. "I remember," she told Brownsteen. Feelings would run high, she thought. She only hoped the demonstrators wouldn't end up hurting their own cause. Accompanied by Ferdi and the detectives who had assisted in the search of Triumph Studios, she headed upstairs to the Fourth Division squad room. She was surprised to find it just about empty.

"Where is everybody?"

The question was directed to Nick Tedesco, who was holding it down. Normally a cheerful person who took what he called the bad in stride, he was very grave. "There was a street shoot-out on Eighty-ninth. A kid was caught in the crossfire. Killed instantly. Briggs and Holden caught it."

When will it end? Norah thought. "Where's Sutphin?" she asked.

Tedesco hesitated. "He went to interview a witness in the García case."

"He has a new lead?"

"That's what he said."

Norah's blue eyes fixed on Tedesco. He was being evasive. The two men were buddies and she sensed Nick was covering for Sutphin. Why? Once he'd fixed on the identity of a perpetrator, Sutphin was inflexible; he didn't allow for any other possibility. In this instance, the García case, Luisa García had confessed. The question was whether she had killed in defense of her mother and herself. Was the threat imminent? That would be settled in court by a jury, but Sutphin had already reached a verdict on his own. The only witness he'd be looking for was one who would support it. Norah's main criticism of Al was that he lacked compassion. She knew very well that his principal criticism of her was that she had too much. Well, that was an ongoing problem. Whatever Tedesco was covering on behalf of his friend couldn't be serious; Nick was an honorable man.

"I want to know when Al calls in," she told him, and continued on to her office.

Where were the reporters? Norah wondered. By now they should certainly have heard about the murder of Ben Russell, brother of a famous rock star. They should be here, swarming, asking questions and demanding answers—which at the moment she didn't have. She'd better make good use of this grace period so that when they finally did show up, she would be ready. Settling herself at her desk, Norah put on her glasses and began to get her thoughts on paper. She typed the heading: "The Rocker case."

Time of death: Indicated by known events: the breakup of the recording session on Tuesday at 11 p.m. and its resumption on Wednesday morning when the artists reassembled beginning at 4:30 a.m. Doc Worgan would narrow it down further.

Access to the studio: So far, only two people were known to have a key.

Motive: As yet no indication as to what it might be. Norah knew very little about Ben Russell. It was limited to what Bo had told her about his professional life and about their relationship. She sensed he had only touched on what was generally known. She needed to go deeper and to explore the relationship with other members of The Earth Shakers.

These people lived in a different world, Norah mused. She didn't understand their lifestyle any better than they did hers, so she must move carefully among them, making sure neither to frighten nor to antagonize. Where should she start?

Leaning back in her chair, Norah took off her glasses

and rubbed the bridge of her nose. As she rested, she became aware of a flickering light in the squad room. Opening her eyes, she saw that the small television set in the far corner was on and Tedesco along with a couple of detectives from downstairs and Ferdi, who had just come in were standing in front of it. Quietly, she joined them.

They were watching the rally at City Hall as it turned into a near riot. According to the commentator, at least ten thousand off-duty cops first tried to storm City Hall, then blocked traffic on the Brooklyn Bridge. The camera panned across a surging mass of humanity. Microphones magnified raucous voices shouting obscenities. There were crudely lettered signs expressing crude sentiments. Sweeping the crowd, the cameras closed in on individual faces flushed with anger and alcohol. One such close-up filled the small screen, and the detectives of the Fourth gasped. Sensing Norah's presence, they turned as one to find out whether the lieut' had seen what they had.

Without a word, she went back to her office.

Unfortunately, she had indeed seen what they had, and they knew it. The worst part was that she wished she hadn't. The problem now was what to do about it. Nothing, she decided. For now. It would depend on the consequences of the rally. Maybe there wouldn't be any. Maybe the whole ugly thing would be written off as a natural reaction by the police to being constantly, and in the main unfairly, criticized by the very people they were trying to help. Cops were only human, after all. They had as much right to blow off steam as anybody. As long as they didn't do it while on duty. That was the crux. She put on her jacket.

"I'm going to the library," she announced on her way out.

Wednesday, September 23
3:30 p.m.

It wasn't the first time Norah Mulcahaney had used the Mid-Manhattan branch on Fifth Avenue between Thirty-ninth and Fortieth to go through back editions of the *New York Times*. She was known by the librarians. Violet Primus in particular was tireless in tracking the material Norah needed. On this occasion, she guided in compiling a history of Bo Russell's career. Using a microreader, Norah made a list of the various awards he had garnered. The reviews and interpretations of his work were almost worshipful. They employed elevated terms: "idiosyncratic style," "disparate musical modes," "stunning dexterity," and—Norah's favorite summation— "His music is dark yet founded on an innate innocence."

Unfamiliar as she was with pop, she would have expected such serious evaluation to be restricted to classical music. To her it seemed pretentious. Clearly, she was a musical illiterate.

Suddenly, without apparent reason, Bo's success express had slowed and then ground to a halt. His concerts were fewer and smaller. His standing in the charts dropped. It was a long fall, and though Bo Russell had spoken casually to Norah about his agent's concern, it was plain that Eleanor Lyras was the one she should talk to next.

Wednesday, September 23
5:00 p.m.

On the basis of Bo Russell's and The Earth Shakers' success, Eleanor Lyras had been able to leave her job with Artists Incorporated, a multi-agent group, and open her own office. On the basis of what she had done for Bo, other artists signed with her. She had a good client list, and though Bo was having hard times, enough commissions were coming in from the others to keep her going. But the big money had dried up.

Lyras's office was in the throbbing center of the music business, Forty-eighth and Eighth. Norah had expected something glamorous—deep carpets, elaborate lighting—but other than a display of the photographs of her famous clients, the office was strictly functional. Somehow, Norah found that reassuring. Ellie Lyras herself, a pretty woman, tall and self-possessed as a Nordic princess, was far from the assertive personality she'd expected.

"I suppose you're here about Ben." Lyras waved Norah to a chair.

"Yes."

"What do you want to know?"

"Why anyone would want to kill him."

The question took the agent aback. "You get right to the point, don't you?"

"It's in everyone's interest to clear this up, isn't it?"

"Oh yes. I certainly agree."

"Let me amend the question. Who do you think killed Ben Russell?"

"Any number of people might have. He wasn't well liked."

"Why not?"

"Many reasons. For one thing, he was Bo's brother. So he had special privileges: He traveled with Bo—in the limo, private car, up front in the charter, whatever. He stayed in the best rooms, same as Bo or at least in better accommodations than the others. Also, he was paid more than the other backup singers. Actually, he worked with

Herb Cranston in the box office when we did a concert, and he also worked with the local P.R. people, so he earned it."

"But the others didn't see it like that," Norah suggested.

"No. They thought he took advantage to further his own career."

"And did he?"

Ellie Lyras shrugged. "He didn't have the talent, so he used other means."

"Was Bo aware of that?"

"Bo looks naive, but he's nobody's fool."

"So he tolerated it."

"They were brothers. Ben practically raised him."

"Yes, Bo told me. So Ben lived better than the others. That's hardly a motive for murder."

The agent was silent for a while. "Ben was a ladies' man. It's no secret. You'll find out soon enough. Seduction was his primary hobby. There wasn't a woman traveling with the group that he hadn't made a play for—usually successfully."

"Wives and girlfriends not excepted?"

"By no means."

"Who was the latest?"

"I can't tell you that, Lieutenant. This kind of thing is ordinary when a group of artists travel together, live and work together. But I'm not on the road with them, so I can't say."

Time to go on, Norah thought. "I understand you discovered Bo Russell?"

A smile lit Lyras's face. "Yes, I did. I was a talent scout for Artists Incorporated at the time. My job was to poke around the small towns, cover the local concerts and clubs. I heard there was a certain millhand church singer. I didn't usually bother with church singers. If the voice was there, they didn't have the *feel* for pop. If they had both the voice and the feel, then probably they'd already taken the next step up and were working the circuit. Then Ben came to see me to pitch his brother. He was very persuasive. I agreed to listen to Bo. In the first eight bars I knew he was the real thing. I forgot all about Ben." She sighed softly.

"Bo was an instant success. The fans took to him right away. There was an electric current that passed between Bo and each individual member in his audience. In the very first year, he won the New York Music Award for debut male vocalist. After that, it was the Artist of the Year award two times running. That's a real big one, you know, because nominees are selected by more than four hundred critics with five finalists in each category. Then the winners are chosen by a combination of critics' votes and the votes of thousands of fans. The rise of his 'Take My Heart' to the top of the charts was stunning. His concerts sold out on the day they were announced."

"What happened?" Norah asked, making no pretense of ignorance about his recent slide.

Lyras sighed. "For one thing—rap. Hip-hop. It captured a whole new audience, but Bo couldn't deal with it. He couldn't absorb it, or integrate it with his own style. He was in constant conflict with it. His forte essentially is a synthesis of folk, rock, and gospel. He's got to go back to it, and that's what he's doing in this new album."

"But he's having trouble?"

Lyras's soft, gray eyes glinted. "What gives you that idea?"

"It's pretty obvious. The rehearsal breaks at eleven. A few hours later, he calls everybody back. Besides, Bo is very forthcoming. He admits the work wasn't going well."

"Bo is a perfectionist. This album could turn his whole career around. Naturally, he wants it to be right."

It struck Norah that they had talked about Bo and that Ben, the victim, was referred to as an afterthought. Even in death, Ben came in second.

"Did Ben have access to Studio A?"

"I don't know," Lyras replied.

"As I understand it, there were only two keys out: Bo had one and Herb Cranston the other. If he didn't have a key, how did Ben get in that night?"

Lyras just shook her head.

"Is it possible he stayed behind after the rehearsal broke at eleven?"

"He could have. I was in the lounge waiting for Bo and I don't recall seeing Ben leave. But I fell asleep and he could have walked right by me without my being aware. You know how it is."

Norah nodded. "Let me ask you this: Have you any idea what Ben might have been doing in the studio after everyone else had left?"

"No. I'm sorry."

"What do you think he might have been doing in the isolation booth?"

"Hiding?" It was neither answer nor question. It was a suggestion.

Norah emerged on the street as the rush hour reached its peak. People spilled off the sidewalks and into the road without regard for traffic, almost daring the motorists to hit them. The buses were jammed; the subways would be too, Norah thought. She could make as good time walking and she liked to walk. Dodging in and out of the ranks of people required her full attention, and it wasn't till she reached Columbus Circle that the crowds thinned. She crossed over to a newsstand outside the park and bought a late edition. The headline stunned her.

DAVE RIPS RALLY COPS' RACIAL SLURS

In much smaller type at the bottom of the page was what she'd been looking for:

ROCK STAR'S BROTHER SHOT
Story on page 5

Norah had expected that Ben Russell's murder would be the lead story and push everything else into the background. But the mayor's reaction and the cops' own behavior kept the rally right up front. The alleged racial slurs could not be ignored. There would be an investigation with big trouble for the officers involved. Every command in the five boroughs would be subjected to the probe.

PROTESTING POLICE LOADED

The accompanying story intimated that the cops were both armed and drinking heavily. That was bad enough, but further on, it was suggested not only that the cops were drinking but that the P.B.A. had paid for the drinks with union credit cards. *God help us!* Norah thought. At least there was no hint in that piece, or in the others, that any but off-duty officers had participated. In fact, scrupulous care was taken to avoid suggesting it. That very caution worried Norah. It indicated to her that they were on the scent of an even bigger story. When they broke it, it would be with plenty of documentation. How would the department respond? Norah was sure that even now Internal Affairs was conducting its own probe to anticipate allegations by the media and to counter them.

What should she do? Norah stood uncertainly in the middle of the sidewalk with people passing in both directions jostling her.

"Wake up, lady! Move it or lose it."

Instinctively, Norah hugged her purse close and felt the reassuring bulk of her service revolver. As she stepped aside, the wind ruffled the open newspaper. She folded it and tossed it into the nearest wastebasket. Why look for trouble? she thought. I.A. might never call her at all. Why not continue to go about her legitimate business? She couldn't be criticized for going directly on to her next interview.

But those who worked in the Big Building had a way of anticipating. When she got to the Park West Hotel, a message was waiting for Lieutenant Mulcahaney. It had been routed through the Fourth, and ordered her to present herself at the office of the C. of D. *forthwith.*

Chapter 7

It was only natural to be nervous when answering a summons from the chief of detectives, Norah thought, but she had never before been afraid of a confrontation either with Chief James Felix, her strong supporter, or with Chief of Detectives Luis Deland, on whose fairness she'd always relied. But on past occasions, she'd been sure of her ground.

Being summoned *forthwith* meant she couldn't even stop for a sandwich. So it was back down into the subway again. As she was going in the opposite direction from the after-work flow, she was at least able to get on a train with reasonable ease and even to find a seat. It was dusk when she reached One Police Plaza.

The crowds had dispersed. Litter, scattered by a fresh wind off the water, was the only trace of the near riot that had taken place there. Sanitation crews were sweeping the debris into carts and emptying them into trucks to be hauled away. The aura of violence lingered.

The Chief's civilian secretary of twenty-two years, Vivian Kamenar, had retired. In the anteroom, a plaque on what had been her desk bore another name: Bella

Newmann. She was young, small, with straight hair cut in a wedge and dyed an unnatural shade of auburn. Norah had never seen her before or even talked to her on the telephone. She was typing. Norah waited for her to stop, but she didn't.

"I'm Lieutenant Mulcahaney." Norah broke in finally. "Fourth Division Homicide. The Chief sent for me."

Bella Newmann continued to the end of the paragraph. Then, without raising her head, she picked up her telephone and punched one of the buttons. "Lieutenant Mulcahaney is here," she announced, and hung up.

"Thank you," Norah said, and started for the Chief's door.

"Not there." Ms. Newmann stopped her. "The auditorium on the ground floor."

"Oh?"

"Chief Deland wants you to look at some news footage. He wants you to see if you recognize anybody."

Norah stood stock-still. She paled. "I'd like to speak to the Chief."

"Commanders are being brought in from all over the city and the boroughs, Lieutenant, to look at the video of the rally and ID any of the men and women they recognize."

Norah swallowed. She was shocked. Deland was asking—no, ordering—them to break the code. "I want to speak to the Chief."

"You can't," Newmann told her bluntly. "He's with the P.C." It was like saying he was with the pope.

So it had already reached the police commissioner, Norah thought. With the mayor's outrage as fuel, it was no wonder.

"I'll wait." Her blue eyes flashing, her blunt jaw thrust forward, Norah wheeled and sat.

First the younger woman gaped. Then she squared her thin shoulders and in a birdlike chirp informed Norah, "Chief Deland specifically ordered that you should view those tapes, Lieutenant. He is not going to be happy when he returns from his meeting with the P.C. and finds out you haven't done it."

Norah remained impassive.

"Captain Jacoby has already been in and has viewed them."

That worried Norah, though she didn't show it. "Good. Then my evidence would be superfluous."

"It was Captain Jacoby who suggested you should be summoned."

Norah caught her breath. Manny Jacoby was her immediate superior. He was a strict disciplinarian and he was also loyal to his people. If he wanted confirmation, it could mean one of two things: he was unsure of his own ID, or he was very sure and wanted backup.

Bella Newmann's eyes were fixed on Norah. "Were you down here earlier today, Lieutenant?"

"No."

"It was an ugly scene. Police officers behaved like hooligans. They shouted obscenities, carried disgusting signs. That's no way to win support for a cause. My father was a cop. More than anything in the world I wanted to be a cop too, but I can't pass the physical."

Norah didn't ask her why. "I'm sorry."

"Those men who carried the signs, they have no right to wear the uniform. They don't deserve the privilege."

"They weren't wearing it at the time," Norah reminded her.

"In uniform or out, they are officers and they have an obligation to behave in a decent and moral manner."

Norah was silent, but she agreed.

"Why don't you go down and look at the tapes, Lieutenant?" Bella Newmann urged more amiably. "You may not see anyone you recognize."

But Norah already knew she would. Unless . . . Unless what she had seen earlier that afternoon with the detectives in the squad room was not part of what had been made available for review by the department. That would present another crisis of conscience. *Stop looking for trouble,* Norah told herself, and nodded to the secretary that she would do it.

The auditorium on the ground floor was used mainly for press conferences and was dark as Norah slipped inside. The television film of the police rally was being run on an oversized screen. By its light Norah was able to see what seats were occupied—a couple dozen, no more. She found a place for herself and sat. As the film rolled, it was interrupted by the occasional call of "Hold!" A frame would be frozen, a close-up followed. There was a brief pause and then the film continued at regular speed.

What would happen to the men and women who were identified? Norah wondered as she sat in the semidarkness watching and listening. How would they be disciplined? With a simple reprimand? A suspension? A drop in rank? When the tape came to an end, it was rewound and started again from the beginning. She watched it through three times. Then she got up and walked the dark aisle to the exit.

She assumed she was expected to go back up to the Chief's office and make a report. Even if she hadn't recognized anyone, a formal report was in order. By not going, she was only postponing the inevitable. The Chief would only reach out for her once more, and he would be annoyed and hardly in the mood to listen to what she had to say. In fact, what arguments could she muster? She could say that in the thick of the mob photographed at the foot of the Brooklyn Bridge she might have recognized one of her own, but she wasn't sure. She could say that, but in truth she *was* sure. She hadn't called for a close-up. She hadn't needed magnification; she hadn't needed the freeze-frame. She knew who it was. She recognized the man from the thickness of his body, from his stance, from the way he held his head tilted slightly to the right. Al Sutphin.

Norah exited the building into the plaza. The sun had set, and a gentle twilight lingered. The streetlights came on. She sat down on a bench to think. If she went away now without reporting to Chief Deland, it would be an act of disobedience. And what would it gain? Time in which someone else might finger Sutphin and get her off the hook. Apparently Captain Jacoby had already identified him and expected her to do the same. She would be hearing from Internal Affairs soon. The matter was already out of her hands.

It wouldn't be Norah's first appearance before the I.A. investigations board either, but in the past she had always testified for the defense. This time it would be not only against another officer but against a member of her own squad. Every instinct opposed it. If only Sutphin had taken part in the demonstration on his own time, she would have been justified in refusing to identify him. But he had been on duty. In fact, he was supposed to have been interrogating the new witness in the García case. Norah remembered only too well that was what he had told Tedesco. And he had been lying.

What disturbed Norah most was that the man she recognized as Detective Al Sutphin appeared to be carrying one of several ugly racist signs. From the camera angle, it was hard to tell whether Sutphin or the man next to him held it. If technicians could blow up the shot enough to show whether or not he was the one, it would count heavily in determining what discipline would be meted out.

Until then it was her duty to stand by him, Norah thought. She got up, crossed Police Plaza, and reentered Police Headquarters.

"We've been looking for you, Lieutenant," Bella Newmann told Norah. "We understood you'd left the building."

"Really?" Norah looked straight at her.

The diminutive secretary studied Norah for a minute. "Obviously, a mistake." She leaned forward to speak into the intercom. "Lieutenant Mulcahaney is here, sir. . . . Go right in," she said to Norah.

Chief James Felix was with Deland. As the C. of D.'s executive officer, he sat in on most meetings. He was a thirty-year veteran. His roan hair had gone completely white; his lantern-jawed face was lean; his green eyes regarded Norah speculatively.

Luis Deland smiled but he didn't wave Norah to a chair. "You have a good look at the video tapes?"

"Yes sir."

"Well? Let's hear it, Lieutenant."

Thursday, September 24
8:00 a.m.

Norah went to work the next morning feeling tired and depressed after a restless night. From the moment she entered the station house she sensed antagonism. It hung thick in the atmosphere. Everyone was busy, too busy to look up and acknowledge her greeting. It was the same in the squad room upstairs. They knew, Norah thought. The word had gotten out. That shouldn't be a surprise; the police grapevine was a marvel of communication, far more efficient than any electronic system. She was barely seated at her desk when there was a tap at the door and Al Sutphin strode in, DD5 report in hand. He slapped it down on the desk blotter. She managed not to jump.

"Report on Mrs. Morales, the new witness in the García case," he said. "For your information, Lieutenant, it was after I finished interrogating Mrs. Morales that I went downtown. By the time I got there I was off duty. You can check the chart. I attended the rally on my own time. I didn't do anything wrong. It's your word against mine."

"I identified you from the film, that's all," Norah countered. "I didn't say what you did or didn't do. I said it was you on the film. That's all. The time the film was shot will fix the time you were at the rally. If what I saw here in the squad was live . . ." She let it hang. "I'm sorry, Al."

"A lot of good that does."

"What else can I say?"

Sutphin scowled. He took a step toward her, his bulk hovering over her. "You'll be a lot sorrier before this is over."

The blood drained from Norah's face. She sat erect, squared her shoulders, and thrust out her jaw.

"Is that a threat?"

"Take it any way you want." Sutphin turned and strode out.

Through the glass of the partition, Norah watched the detectives gather round Sutphin. There was conversation, some backslapping, and after surreptitious glances in her direction, all returned to their desks. Norah was dejected. She had always supported her people. This was the first time she'd been forced to go against one of her own.

As the squad room settled into an uneasy silence, Norah studied Sutphin's report. He had canvassed the neighborhood where the Garcías lived and worked. He'd gotten nowhere, but he hadn't given up. He examined the record of calls to 911 on the morning of the break-in and murder. In doing so, he discovered there had been more than one report of the violence in the stationery store. Luisa García had called; they knew that. But before her call, there was one from a certain Rosa Morales to report the violence. Luisa García's confession of murder had wiped out the earlier complaint. Nobody had bothered to follow up on it till Sutphin. He had been smart and professional, Norah thought, and nobody could accuse him of settling for the easy solution, not this time.

Four or five minutes passed and she was deep into the report when there was another tap at the door. This time it was Ferdi.

With a warm smile, she waved him in.

He entered, closed the door behind him, but was too preoccupied to smile back. "There's a lot of bad feeling out there, Norah." His using her first name there, in the office, indicated his concern.

"Tell me about it!" she snapped.

"Sorry, Lieutenant." He started to leave.

"Wait, Ferdi. I didn't meant to take your head off, but you've got to understand . . . I had no choice. You were here when we saw Al on TV. It was after four. If what we saw was live, then he was off duty and in the clear." She made no mention of the sign he might or might not have been carrying; that was another matter. "I called the network," she continued. "They told me it was a tape replay of a segment shot at noon. So he was on duty."

"I'll tell them." Arenas nodded toward the detectives outside who, while apparently engrossed in their work, were covertly watching the exchange between their commanding officer and her whip. "You've said that you're opposed to a review board composed entirely of civilians."

"That's right. I am."

"You also claim to support the right of police officers to demonstrate just as civilians do."

"On their own time."

"To them, that's a technicality. They . . . We count on you to support us."

"Haven't I always?"

"Did you have to make a positive ID?" Ferdi exclaimed. "Why couldn't you just have said you weren't sure?"

Norah looked at him with disappointment. "Because I *was* sure."

"There are times, Lieutenant, when you need to shave the truth."

"I'm surprised to hear that from you, Sergeant."

"I've learned a few things over the years."

"The wrong things, it seems."

"Times have changed and you have to adapt to survive. You're an idealist, Norah. You can afford to be. Most of us have obligations."

Norah's blue eyes flashed. "What Sutphin and the cops with him did was a shame to all of us."

"It was also done for all of us," Ferdi Arenas pointed out.

"What do you want from me?" Norah cut to the core. "Al Sutphin is a veteran with a good record. I'm not trying to take any of that away from him." She looked down at the report he'd placed in front of her and which she hadn't finished studying. "But what he did was wrong and it wasn't even smart. I'm sorry, but I can't change my testimony."

Ferdi sighed heavily. "This is going to have bad consequences," he warned. "There's a clique against you. You've given the people who don't like you something tangible to complain about. They're going to make trouble."

"There are always some who are jealous, who resent success. You and I both know about that."

He saw that he wouldn't be able to convince her. "If you need me, all you have to do is say so."

Their eyes met. "Thank you, Ferdi."

Norah understood that as her friend of many years and her trusted aide, Ferdi Arenas had been delegated to approach her. She was not surprised he'd accepted the job. He might have reasoned that he could present their complaint in a way that wouldn't hurt so much, but she was surprised that he seemed to believe in the arguments he'd put forward. It took her back some fifteen years to an earlier job action by police.

That had been in protest over a new contract and had been spread out for weeks. The men had marched on Gracie Mansion, a rowdy bunch swilling beer, shouting, banging on metal trash cans, disturbing the peace of the neighborhoods they passed through. On September 28—a date that was etched in her memory, the occasion of the Ali-Norton fight—on-duty cops had confronted their off-duty brothers at a packed Yankee Stadium. Norah had been on Radio Motor Patrol duty. On October 6, the opening of the hockey season, cops demonstrated outside Madison Square Garden. That resulted in two suspensions, and the next day a hundred policemen marched on City Hall to protest the suspensions. It snowballed. In eighteen precincts of Manhattan, Brooklyn, and the Bronx, on-duty cops left the transmitting buttons of their walkie-talkies open, thus jamming police frequencies and risking the safety of their brother officers.

Norah recalled how appalled Ferdi had been, yet his support and respect for the department was never shaken. Now he was wavering. Not only was he siding with the demonstrators but he was justifying their behavior. Forcing herself to block out the past, Norah returned to Al Sutphin's report.

The witness Sutphin had turned up, Rosa Morales, was a nurse on night duty at Presbyterian. She was coming home from work and had just entered her apartment, which overlooked the García store. She was getting ready to go to bed and was at the window in the act of pulling down the blind, when she noticed a man inside the store. He had his back to her. It was too early for the store to be open, so he couldn't have been a customer. Norah read through the rest of it, then went back through it once again. Finally she went out into the squad room and approached Sutphin at his desk.

"According to this, the witness didn't see the actual trashing of the premises."

Looking up, Sutphin met Norah's gaze directly. "That's correct. By the time Mrs. Morales got home, that part of it was all over. The man she saw was just standing there, not moving, facing Mrs. García, who wasn't moving either. The witness then heard three shots. Mrs. García screamed. The man went down. Unfortunately, the witness couldn't identify him, as he had his back to her throughout."

"We know it was Ricardo García."

"Do we?"

Norah was shocked. "Are you suggesting someone other than the son broke in?"

"Could be. Could be somebody he owed broke in, took what he could carry, trashed what he couldn't. Ricardo arrived after it was all over."

"For heaven's sake! Mrs. García herself admits it was her son."

Sutphin shrugged. "Sure. She's looking to save her daughter. You should know. You showed her how to do it."

Behind her, the men gasped. Norah felt the blood surge and knew her cheeks flamed. "And you intend to show there was no immediate threat to either the mother or the sister. You intend to show Luisa García shot without direct provocation—in other words, that it was premeditated murder. Okay. I'll make sure your report gets to the Chief. It will be up to him to pass it on to the D.A."

"I don't need any favors from you, Lieutenant."

"It's no favor. You're entitled."

"You should have thought of that before you turned me in."

The silence rang in Norah's ears. All pretense of working was gone. There wasn't a man in the room who wasn't watching and waiting for Norah's response.

"You should have thought of the consequences of attending the rally. But then I don't suppose you expected to get caught. You ought at least to have the courage of your convictions."

Sutphin paled. Slowly, he got out of the chair and lumbered around the desk to face Norah. His hands, clenched and held rigidly at his sides, trembled.

Ferdi tensed, took a step forward, and prepared to intervene.

Norah held her ground and prayed she wouldn't flinch.

"You're lucky you're a woman," Sutphin said. Then he turned abruptly, reached for his jacket hanging over the back of the chair, and walked out of the room.

Norah didn't move till he was gone. "If anyone has something to say, now's the time." She made a long, slow visual sweep of those present. It would take only one remark to get the ball rolling that could very well start an avalanche of insurrection. She waited. Ferdi was the first to turn and go back to his desk. One by one, the others did the same. Norah waited till everyone was seated before returning to her office and closing the door. Her heart was pounding.

Ferdi was right. She'd had no idea feelings were running so high. Sutphin's resentment was to be expected, yet she couldn't believe that even that was based solely on her identification of him on the tape. He had never liked her, had never really accepted her as his superior. They'd had a few minor run-ins; at least, they'd been minor to her. She knew such things had a way of building. What shocked her was the reaction of the others. From them she had expected full support. Propping her elbows on the desk, Norah cradled her head in her hands.

Thursday, September 24
8:00 p.m.

She hadn't eaten all day, so when she got home the first thing Norah did was make a peanut butter sandwich which she washed down with a glass of orange juice. Then she got into pajamas and slippers, turned on the television, and stretched out on the sofa. A special news program was presenting the scene of the police rally she had viewed earlier downtown. She let it run till the phone rang. She turned down the volume, but kept watching.

"Yes?"

No answer.

"Hello? Who's calling?"

No answer.

"Who is this? What do you want?" Norah persisted. "Say what you have to say now, or I'm hanging up."

"You're not wanted. You don't belong. Get out. Resign while you still can."

The line went dead.

Norah sat there, frozen. Who could it be? Who disliked her enough to do this? She was more angry than frightened. She hadn't recognized the voice; it was muffled, disguised.

The phone rang again. She snatched it up quickly. "You can't scare me. I'm not resigning, so forget about it."

"Lieutenant Mulcahaney?" a light voice, a woman's delicate voice, queried.

It took a moment for Norah to realize who it was. "Sister Beatrice? Is that you? I'm sorry. I thought . . . I'm sorry. How are you?"

"I'm fine. More to the point, how are you?"

"All right. Honestly. I just had one of those crank calls. A heavy breather. You know."

"Fortunately, I don't. Well, I have some good news. A six-month-old infant has become available. The mother had wanted to keep her, but she's too sick to cope. Would you be interested?"

"Oh yes! Would I be interested? Oh, Sister, yes!" Every anxiety fell away and was forgotten.

"I thought you might be. When can you come over to see her?"

"It's a girl. Oh, it's a girl! How wonderful! I can come now. Right now."

The nun laughed softly. "Tomorrow will be time enough. Can you make it tomorrow morning at, say, nine?"

"I'll be there. I'll be there at nine promptly. And thank you, Sister. Thank you so much."

Chapter 8

Holding the infant in her arms, Norah felt a surge of love so strong it hurt. "What's her name?"

"Maryanne."

"Maryanne," Norah repeated. "Oh, Sister, she's the most beautiful baby I've ever seen."

Sister Beatrice smiled indulgently. "Then I take it you'd like to make a formal application to adopt?"

"Of course."

"All right, let's go fill out the papers."

Reluctantly, Norah relinquished the baby to the waiting paraprofessional. "I'll see you soon, sweetheart," she said, and followed Sister Beatrice back to her office. "I thought I'd already filled out an adoption request," she said when the sheaf of documents was placed in front of her.

"That was just a general application. This is for a specific child."

Norah got to it. When she was finished, she handed over the papers. "When will I be able to have her?"

"As soon as the investigation is completed."

"What investigation?"

"We have to verify that what you say in this application is true, and that you are emotionally and financially fit to take on this responsibility."

Norah blanched. "I thought you already did that."

"Not in detail. Have you any idea, Lieutenant, how many people walk in here wanting to adopt? If we conducted a close investigation of each one, we wouldn't have time to do anything else. Or money. You know what's involved—who better? So we check the address where they say they live and we check that they actually work where they say they do, and that gets them on the list. When a child becomes available, then we really look them over."

"I see."

"I don't think you have anything to worry about, Lieutenant."

"Thank you."

"You'll be hearing from me."

Norah stood up. "You won't offer her to anybody else, will you?"

"Not unless you're turned down."

And Norah had to be satisfied with that.

But Norah's natural optimism overcame her anxiety. By the time she got back uptown to the station house, she had convinced herself that all would be well both with the adoption and with the Sutphin problem. When she entered, she was accorded a nod here and there, a casual greeting—nothing overwhelming but certainly an improvement over yesterday's coldness. According to news reports, a steady stream of cops who had been identified by their superiors as having been present at Wednesday's rally and behaving in a manner that dishonored the department were being interrogated by I.A. As far as Norah knew, and she was sure someone would have been pleased to tell her otherwise, Al Sutphin was not one of those summoned. On entering the squad room, the first thing Norah did was look to see if he was at his desk. He was. Their eyes met briefly. Norah moved on.

In her office, the first thing she saw was a large white envelope lying on the center of her desk blotter. Her name was printed on it in thick black letters probably drawn with a Magic Marker. She approached it warily.

She picked it up; nothing happened. Holding it at arm's length, she lifted the flap. Nothing. She laughed weakly and sat down. It was farfetched for a letter bomb to be delivered to her inside the police station. But a while back a fire bomb had been planted in one of the precinct houses and successfully ignited. There had been no loss of life, but plenty of heavy structural damage. Before removing the single sheet of paper in the envelope, Norah debated calling the bomb squad. Actually, it would be the proper and prudent way to handle this. On the other hand, if it was a dud she'd look like a coward—or worse, a fool. She couldn't afford anything that would make her look incompetent and unable to handle her responsibilities or might reflect on her qualifications to adopt. That had now become Norah's main concern. So, holding the sheet between thumb and forefinger, she carefully drew it out of the envelope. The message was in the same crude lettering and done with the same type of marker as her name on the envelope. The words jumped at her.

WATCH YOUR BACK

She whirled around, but nobody was there.

False alarm? A bad joke? Looking out through the glass of the partition, she couldn't see anyone in the squad room laughing. Nobody was even looking her way. The panic dissolved into anger. Holding paper and envelope, she strode out.

"Who put this on my desk?"

Blank looks.

"How did it get on my desk? It didn't walk in by itself."

"It could have been delivered by messenger," Ferdi suggested, puzzled by her tone.

"And nobody saw him? A stranger just walked in through a roomful of detectives and nobody stopped him? Nobody asked what he was doing?"

"What's up, Lieutenant?" Ferdi asked quietly.

"Call down and ask Sergeant Brownsteen if he authorized anybody to make a delivery."

Arenas picked up the phone. "Did anyone come in this morning with a letter for Lieutenant Mulcahaney? . . . You're sure? . . . Okay, thanks." He hung up. "He says not, Lieutenant."

"If it wasn't brought in by someone from outside, then it was brought by someone already inside. There's no other choice."

"Just exactly what are we being accused of, Lieutenant?" Al Sutphin asked.

She pondered the question. "Maybe only a bad sense of humor. I hope that's all." The ring of the telephone in her office put an end to the discussion. She hurried inside to answer.

"Homicide. Lieutenant Mulcahaney."

"Jim Felix, Norah."

"Oh. Good morning, Chief." This was it, she thought. This was the order to send Sutphin down for interrogation and probably to come herself. On the other hand, no, she thought. Jim Felix was a three-star chief; he wouldn't be making this kind of summons himself. He had underlings for that.

"What have you got on the Rocker case?" Felix asked.

Hard to believe, but she'd almost forgotten about it. "Not much. I've been tied up with that other business."

"Forget it," he told her. "They're not going to call you. They've got enough alleged participants to interrogate, for now anyway. Chief Deland wants you to give the Rocker case top priority."

"Yes sir." If she was off the hook, that meant Sutphin was too. Norah felt her tension ease.

"Have you seen the morning papers?"

"Not yet."

"The media is shifting attention from the rally to the murder. We want to encourage that. We don't want to appear so wrapped up in dissension that we can't take care of business."

"No sir."

"Bo Russell is a big star. The murder of his brother is bound to be more interesting to the public than a union rally."

"We'll get right on it, Chief."

"Good. And one more thing, Norah . . ."

"Sir?"

"Are you having a disciplinary problem up there?"

"A disciplinary problem? Here? No sir."

"I didn't think so." James Felix paused. "If you do need help though, anytime . . . you'll be sure to let me know?"

"I certainly will." Message received and understood, Norah thought as she put the phone down.

So, for the time being at least, both she and Al Sutphin could get back to normal. She brought out the file she'd started on the Rocker case. Leafing through it, she picked up the threads of what had been done so far and what was next. She considered which of her squad should be picked to form a task force. There was Ferdi, of course; he was the whip, the one who got things done. Simon Wyler's broad interests ensured that he would deal sympathetically with the musicians and artists. Julius Ochs would examine the financial aspects.

And then there was Sutphin. She walked out to him.

"Anything new on the García case?"

"Like what?"

"Like a witness who actually saw something, maybe one of the earlier incidents that terrorized the mother and sister?"

"According to the García women, the guy the kid brought with him was a professional enforcer. You think he did his number in front of witnesses? Come on, Lieutenant."

"If he wanted to throw a scare into the other store owners in the neighborhood . . ."

"Then he succeeded. Let me tell you, Lieutenant, not one of those people is going to talk. I've interviewed every single owner, resident, and anybody who has any business on that block twice over. Nobody's going to open his mouth. They're scared shitless."

Norah hesitated. If she included Sutphin on the Rocker team, it could be seen as a peace offering, an admission that she had broken the code by identifying him. In addition, Sutphin had trouble at home. His wife had left him, taking the children. His mind was divided. No, she decided, Sutphin would be a source of unrest, a negative influence.

"Keep trying," she said.

He scowled. He knew the Rocker case was hot and would be taking precedence. He also knew Norah Mulcahaney had just passed him over in making the assignments. "Excuse me, Lieutenant, but it's a waste of time."

"I'll decide that," she retorted.

Norah encouraged her people to air their grievances,

and Sutphin seemed on the verge of speaking out. His face darkened; he tightened like a spring coiling; again he seemed to present a physical threat. Then suddenly, without another word, he turned from her and resumed typing.

Norah passed on. She pointed to the men she wanted and indicated they were to go into her office.

Arenas, Wyler, and Ochs settled in their accustomed places established after a number of such meetings.

"The chief wants us to give the Rocker case top priority."

The announcement was received with satisfaction. They exchanged smiles with one another and with Norah. Working together was the best way of healing dissension, Norah thought. For a moment she considered calling Sutphin in after all, but she didn't. If he was the one who called her home last night and left the note on her desk this morning, she would not buy him off.

"I don't see throwing the whole squad at these people. I don't want them intimidated. They're artists. They live in a world of their own. They have their own unique way of looking at things. I want them to trust us and cooperate with us. Ben Russell was found murdered in the isolation booth of a recording studio. Whether he was killed there or put there afterward, we don't know yet. Actually, what we've got here is a version of a locked room puzzle. To solve the crime we have to know why it was committed in that particular place. That should lead us to the motive."

She paused, giving them time to digest what she'd said.

"I've talked to Eleanor Lyras, Bo's agent as well as Ben's. According to Ms. Lyras, the brothers were close, but the rest of the group wasn't crazy about Ben. Besides singing backup, Ben was also involved in the business end of The Earth Shakers. He helped check box office receipts at the end of a concert performance. I get the impression from Lyras that Ben might have had sticky fingers. Julie, I want you to look into that."

Detective Second Grade Julius Ochs beamed. He made no secret of his ambition. He was twenty-five, sallow, almost puny. In fact, he'd barely survived the physical training requirements. He would rise by way of civil service exams rather than action on the streets. Nevertheless, he worked out at the gym three times a week. Of course, he was attending John Jay College. He had just completed a course in accounting, so he was delighted with the assignment.

"Again according to Lyras," Norah continued, "Ben Russell was known to be a womanizer. He'd had every woman in the group, married or single. He also sampled the local talent while on the road."

"That must have made him a few enemies," Simon Wyler observed in his usual wry manner. Wyler always presented an elegant figure. Today he wore a fine Italian vested suit cut close to his lean frame.

"I expect you to find out," Norah told him while the others grinned.

It wasn't a man's good qualities that got him killed, Norah thought, so it made sense to home in on those who had disliked the victim. They would be the ones most willing to reveal his dark side. In Ben Russell's case, it would be a long list. Herb Cranston would be at the top of it, she decided. As manager of The Earth Shakers, he couldn't have been too pleased to have the boss's brother looking over his shoulder.

The Park West Hotel was just a few blocks away from the station house. Norah and Ferdi walked over. Checking at the desk, they found Cranston was in his room. They were announced and went up.

Jacket off, shirtsleeves rolled up, a pencil clamped between his teeth, the manager met them at the door. A portable computer was on the desk with piles of papers on either side and on every available surface. The room was small. It might not have seemed so cramped if it weren't for the disorder. Cranston looked in vain for somewhere for the police officers to sit.

"I'll call down for a couple of folding chairs."

"Thank you," Norah said.

That put him momentarily off balance. He hadn't expected her to accept. He'd thought she would tell him not to bother, they wouldn't be there long, that there were only a couple of points they needed to clear up. He tried to hide his anxiety.

"May I offer you some coffee? Tea? Anything at all?"

"No, thanks." Norah wanted the wait to be awkward; she didn't want it relieved. When the chairs were delivered at last and the bellboy had been tipped, everybody sat.

"We're curious to know just how much help Ben Russell was to you," Norah began.

"Help?"

"Yes. I take it Bo wanted his brother to learn the business side of the music business, but as the boss's brother he could have been a nuisance."

"I see what you mean." Cranston relaxed a bit. "No, Ben didn't bother me, mainly because he wasn't particularly interested."

"I understand one of his jobs was to help check box office receipts after a concert. I assume he was under supervision."

"Of course."

"Could he somehow have skimmed the profits? Cooked the books?"

Cranston shook his head. "He wasn't that smart, Lieutenant." He paused. "I had my eye on him."

"But he lived well," Norah pointed out. "On the same level as Bo, more or less."

"Bo insisted on it. He paid for it."

"On the road, yes, but how about at home?"

"Same thing. Bo bought his brother a home on a par with his and in the same area. In that way, each retained his privacy but was within easy call of the other. All of Ben's bills were sent to me."

"It sounds like his salary was pocket money. Very nice. What did he spend it on?" Norah waited, but it seemed Cranston needed to be prompted. "Was he into drugs? Gambling?"

"Women." Cranston's broad face showed his disapproval. "He used them and when he got bored, he tossed them aside. They didn't all go quietly."

"Ah . . ." Norah sighed. She looked to Ferdi and then back to the manager. "I take it you have someone particular in mind. Tell us about her."

Cranston nodded. "Daisy Barth. A beautiful girl, dark hair, face of an angel. Of course, she was a virgin then, and young—seventeen. That's the way Ben liked them. He was lucky she wasn't younger—that would have been real trouble. It wouldn't have stopped him, though. Once he felt the itch, he had to satisfy it."

"What happened?"

"The girl got pregnant. What else? Ben denied responsibility. He made some ugly counteraccusations. The girl's father went to Bo, of course. And Bo paid off. He paid the girl's medical expenses and made her a living allowance. It was supposed to support her till she was able to go back to work."

"It seems there was no end to Bo's generosity as far as his brother was concerned," Norah remarked.

"I'm not so sure," Cranston replied. "Bo read his

brother the riot act on that one. He really chewed Ben out. Told him the next time he'd have to marry the girl."

"So Daisy Barth had an abortion and that was the end of it," Norah concluded.

"No. She wanted the baby."

"I see. And then?"

"Nothing. She had it. She collects her checks and that's it. We don't hear from her. Ben's lucky again—she could have been a leech on him for the rest of his life."

"Was it a boy or a girl?"

Cranston shrugged.

"Nobody cared enough to find out?" Norah didn't hide her disapproval. "How long ago did all this take place?"

"I'd say she gave birth about six months ago. I can check."

"Not necessary. No other involvements since?"

"As far as I know, nothing serious. Of course, with Ben you couldn't be sure."

"Where is Daisy Barth now?"

"At home with her father, I suppose."

"In Bethlehem?"

He nodded.

"So she was a hometown girl."

"That's right." He was silent for several moments. "You're not going to stir all this up again, are you, Lieutenant?"

"Why should you care?"

"For Bo's sake. The publicity would be bad. Things haven't been going well lately. He needs to keep his focus on this new album."

"There's a better chance of his keeping his focus once the murder of his brother is solved, don't you think?"

"Of course. You're right."

Norah got up and so did Ferdi.

"One more question, Mr. Cranston. What do you think Ben Russell was doing in Studio A in the middle of the night?"

Sweat broke out on the manager's broad forehead. Damp patches appeared on his shirt.

"I wish to God I knew," he said.

Chapter 9

"If Cranston didn't want us to investigate Daisy Barth, why did he tell us about her?" Ferdi wondered while he and Norah stood in the corridor waiting for the elevator.

"It draws our attention away from Bo," Norah pointed out. "It offers new suspects not connected to Bo or The Earth Shakers. By saying he hopes we don't dig it all up again, he suggests there's more to the affair than appears. It's his way of protecting Bo."

"Everybody wants to protect Bo."

Before Norah could comment, the elevator arrived. There were other passengers, so the conversation was suspended. They got off at the lobby and by common accord headed outside.

"Want a hot dog?" Ferdi had spotted a vendor.

"I'd love one."

They crossed the street, bought their franks, and settled on a bench on the outside of the park wall. They ate the first few bites in silence.

"Do you think Bo killed his brother?" Ferdi asked.

"Everything we've heard so far indicates Bo cared deeply for his older brother. He let him get away with just about anything till the trouble with Daisy."

They continued to munch.

"I don't think Ben expected Bo to react so violently to the girl's pregnancy. He promised he'd behave himself, but my guess is, it wasn't for long. But if he wasn't good, he must at least have learned to be careful."

"Why do you suppose that particular affair bothered Bo so much more than the others, assuming there were others?" Ferdi asked.

"I think we can assume that. Apparently, Daisy's wanting to have her child touched Bo and scared Ben. My guess is, it didn't scare him enough."

"You think he got another woman in trouble?"

"Got himself into trouble is more likely." Finishing the last of her hot dog, Norah wiped her lips with the paper napkin and tossed it into a nearby wastebasket. "Let's go find out."

Friday, September 25
1:30 p.m.

Duggie Watts and Rollo Dubois were still in the room. In fact, they were just getting up; they hadn't dressed yet, nor shaved. The beds were unmade. Room service had delivered a late brunch—fried eggs, bacon, and a stack of buttered toast—which they were demolishing. Duggie Watts answered the knock.

"Morning, Lieutenant. Morning, Sergeant. Oh, I guess it's afternoon," he corrected himself cheerfully. "Come on in, anyway. Care for something? Coffee? Whatever? We can send down."

"We just ate, thanks," Norah answered.

"Mind if we go ahead?" Without waiting for an answer, Watts returned to the table and sat opposite Dubois.

The roommates wore matching Japanese-style velour

robes. Watts's was burgundy. As he leaned forward to put the fork into his mouth, it fell open to reveal dark chest hair. Dubois's was royal blue. Watts's robe was too long for him and made him look like a gnome. Dubois's was too short and exposed knobby knees and spindly legs. They were one-size-fits-all items that fit nobody, Norah thought.

"Don't let us keep you from your breakfast," she said, though both already had their mouths full. She took a chair and Ferdi followed suit. "There are a couple of points we didn't cover at the studio. We think maybe you can help us."

"We'll try." Watts continued as spokesman, between mouthfuls.

"Have you any idea who might have wanted to kill Ben Russell?"

Watts stopped chewing. "Line forms to the right, Lieutenant."

"He wasn't liked?"

"You could put it like that." Watts helped himself to more toast.

"It takes more than dislike to make somebody commit murder."

"True." Watts spread jam on the toast.

Norah looked to Rollo Dubois, whose mouth was also full and who merely nodded his agreement. She returned to Watts. "You can do better than that."

"Right." He finished the eggs, wiped the plate with a piece of toast, and freshened his coffee. "Ben made a play for every woman he ever met regardless of whether she had a boyfriend or was married, and whether she was interested or not. If he hadn't been Bo's brother, the guys would have beat him up and kicked him where it hurts. Seems finally somebody got the guts to take action."

"Who?"

"I have no idea. If I had, I wouldn't tell you. Whoever it was, he did everybody a favor."

"I understand, but I am going to find out."

"Fine. But not from me."

Norah looked at Dubois.

"Not from me," he echoed.

"At least tell me who his latest girlfriend was. Come on, guys, don't you want to see the killer caught?"

Watts replied. "I'm not so sure. Suppose we give you a name and it turns out to be a mistake?"

"We're not looking to railroad anybody. I understand he had a girl here in New York."

"He had a girl in every town, big and small. Honestly, that's all we know."

Norah waited a beat. "How about Daisy Barth?" She threw the name out casually. "Ever hear about her?"

"She's ancient history."

"How so?"

Watts shrugged. "Bo paid her off."

"How many others did he pay off?"

"I don't think there's a count."

Norah nodded; then, without laying a foundation, she shifted abruptly. "What do you suppose Ben was doing in the isolation booth in the middle of the night?"

Watts was not taken aback. In fact, he grinned. His dark eyes threw off sparks of mischief. "That's easy. You shouldn't need to ask, Lieutenant. He was making it with some girl. Well, not in the booth—that would have been a little crowded—but for sure that's why he was in the studio. He met most of his dates in the studio after a session. Or if we were in concert, it would be backstage in one of the dressing rooms, preferably Bo's. The women were excited to be doing it in Bo's dressing room."

"Did he know?"

Watts smirked. "Everybody else did."

It had the ring of truth and it made sense, Norah thought. It fit the emerging portrait of the victim. "Why didn't you tell me this before?"

"You didn't ask. Besides, I didn't want to embarrass Bo."

If Bo had known what his brother was using the studios and dressing rooms for, as well he might have, he could have put a stop to it easily. Also, a big point had been made about the studio not being accessible to anyone without a key. Ben must have gone to the trouble of having one duplicated.

"How long have you been with the group?" Norah asked Watts.

"From the start, or close enough. When he organized The Earth Shakers, Bo took on as many of his buddies from his hometown as he could. If they had no particular talent to sing or play an instrument, he gave them jobs on the crew. I was taking a course in electronics at the time. Bo urged me to concentrate on sound engineering. When I finished, he hired me as his personal mix engineer."

"He's loyal to his friends," Norah observed.

"And we stick by him."

"I can see that. Didn't Bo ever object to Ben's behavior? Didn't he ever lose his temper?"

"Only one time over Daisy. That I know of."

"How about the rest of the family? Is Bo good to them?"

"There's nobody else. Their father, Jim Russell, was killed in a mill accident. Jessie Russell, their mother, committed suicide a year later. She was devastated by her husband's death. Hung herself. Ben came home from school one day and found her. He was fourteen. He went to a neighbor's house for help, but first he made sure to lock the door of the room she was in so that Bo wouldn't walk in on her the way he did."

That was not the story Bo had told, Norah thought, and she could well understand why.

"I'm told there was an aunt."

"Right, the mother's sister, but she had three kids of her own. She wasn't interested in taking on two more. I'll bet she wishes now that she had."

So far everybody Norah and Ferdi had talked to agreed on the explanation of the tie between the brothers. Bo felt he owed his older brother and never stopped trying to pay him back. Ben never stopped taking. It was time to talk to somebody who might see things from Ben's point of view, Norah thought. She knew of only one such person—Bo himself.

She rang the star's suite from the lobby. A woman answered.

"This is Lieutenant Mulcahaney. I'd like to speak to Mr. Russell, please."

"I'm sorry, Bo isn't here."

"Is this Mrs. Russell?" Norah asked. "I wonder if Sergeant Arenas and I might come up and speak with you?"

The woman hesitated. "Actually, this isn't a good time. I'm not feeling well."

"I'm sorry to hear that. When will Mr. Russell be back?"

"I don't know. He didn't say. He went for a walk."

"How long ago was that?"

"Maybe an hour. I'm not sure. It's hard to say when he'll be back. He loses track of time. He'll go into a movie and sit through a couple of showings without realizing it."

"I understand. When he comes in, please ask him to call me. He has my number."

Gloria Russell wavered. "I suppose . . . if it's important, you could come up. If you want?"

"Thank you, Mrs. Russell." Norah hung up quickly before Gloria Russell could change her mind. Together she and Ferdi went directly up to the twelfth floor, but were kept waiting a considerable time after knocking—so long that Norah thought the lady had indeed decided against seeing them after all. Then the door opened just a crack.

"Mrs. Russell?" Norah peered through. "I'm Lieutenant Mulcahaney and this is Sergeant Arenas. I just spoke to you on the phone from the lobby. May we come in?"

The first thing Norah noticed about Gloria Russell when she reluctantly let them in was that she was certainly older than Bo and probably older than Ben. The second was that although it was still early in the day, she'd already had a couple of drinks. She was a beautiful, voluptuous woman. Her hair was a bleached platinum cloud around a dead-white face. Her eyes were large and dark and her lashes were heavy with black mascara. Her lips were glossy, painted into a childish pout. Her complexion was unlined. A closer inspection suggested that was due to collagen injections currently popular and to a steady consumption of alcohol which puffed up her entire face. As she couldn't see a glass or bottle around, Norah concluded Gloria Russell was already practiced in the art of hiding her habit and that was why she and Ferdi had been kept waiting. She wasn't bothering to hide anything else, Norah thought. She was wearing a see-through gauze negligee of varying shades ranging from shell pink to flaming orange. The backlighting from the picture window that overlooked the park revealed that under the negligee Mrs. Russell wore the tiniest of lace bikinis. Norah looked at Ferdi and bit back a smile: He was blushing.

This was the sitting room of the suite, the best the Park West Hotel had to offer, Norah had no doubt, but it was not exactly the equal of the Plaza or the Waldorf. An attempt had been made to dress it up: Flowers were everywhere in huge bouquets so perfectly symmetrical they seemed unreal. Piles of throw pillows were intended to disguise the drab upholstery.

"This is where Bo stayed the first time he came to New York," Gloria Russell explained. "He was living here, not in a suite, naturally, when he cut his first record. Now, when we come to New York, he won't stay anywhere else. He's very superstitious."

She was apologizing for the modesty of the accommodations, Norah realized. "I can understand that."

"You can?" Evidently Gloria could not.

"It wasn't so long ago."

"Six years."

"And you've been married . . . how long?"

"Five."

"Any children?"

"No."

And time was running out, Norah thought—that is, if she was interested in having children.

"How did you and Bo meet?"

"Why? Why do you want to know?"

Norah was surprised at the strong reaction to what had been a casual question. She had a hunch. "You met through Ben, didn't you?"

"So?"

"It's Ben I'm interested in. How well did you know him?"

Gloria Russell licked her already shining lips. She reached for a cigarette from a Lucite box on a side table and lit it with a shaking hand. "You know how well. Don't pretend someone hasn't already told you all about it."

Norah looked at her long and hard. "As a matter of fact, no. No one we've talked to has mentioned any connection between you and your husband's brother. Nobody has even mentioned your name."

The singer's wife took a couple of quick drags on the cigarette. It didn't calm her. She ground it out in the nearest ashtray and strode over to a closed cabinet. Opening it, she reached for a highball glass, half filled, the ice in it just about melted. With a practiced hand she added a generous shot from a bottle of Dewar's and knocked it off in one desperate swallow. Her need was greater than her desire to keep the secret.

"I don't think you were the one they were trying to protect."

A smile twisted the painted lips. "It's always Bo."

"Why?"

"He pays their salaries. He keeps them alive. Do you know why things are going so bad for Bo right now? I'll tell you why. It's because of the no-talent bunch he keeps around him."

"Why should they think he needs protection?" Norah pressed. "Do they think he killed his brother? Might it have been over you?"

Gloria Russell finished off her drink, then with a steadier hand poured herself another. This she took in small gulps.

"You flatter me, Lieutenant. I was Ben's girlfriend first. That was way back when Bo was just the kid brother who sang in church on Sunday. Bo had a big crush on me, but he was so young! Well, actually there was only six years between them, but it seemed like a lot more. I was crazy for Ben, but Ben wasn't interested in any kind of permanent relationship." She shrugged. "Then one day this talent scout from New York, Eleanor Lyras, came to town. Ben went to see her. He wanted her to audition Bo. He was very persuasive."

That wasn't quite the way Ms. Lyras had told it, Norah reflected. Shadings and modulations depended on who was telling the story.

"Once she heard him, Lyras signed him to an exclusive contract, and you know the rest. 'Take My Heart' was the first hit. He dedicated it to me. I was touched, naturally. I thought it was sweet. I certainly wasn't prepared for it to go over the way it did. It was a phenomenal success. I mean, everybody was either singing or playing the song. I heard it on radio, on MTV. The record hit the top of the charts. . . . And all of it was directed at me. It was like all those people were singing to me. It made me feel like a celebrity myself, you know?"

A faraway look came into her dark eyes. "Then Bo went to Ben and asked him what his intentions were regarding me. Ben said he had no intentions." The light died, but only for a moment. "Then Bo asked him if in that case he'd mind if he, Bo, asked me to marry him. Can you believe that? Bo actually asked permission!"

Norah didn't know what to say, but apparently a comment wasn't expected.

"Ben told him to go ahead." Her mood changed. "He handed me over like merchandise. I mean, it was insulting. I was mad. Real mad. So when Bo proposed, I said yes. Right away."

Would she have said no otherwise? Norah wondered.

"We had a real gorgeous wedding. All the top stars came. Bruce Springsteen was there. Can you imagine—Bruce Springsteen was at my wedding! All the newspapers and magazines covered it. We were on the front page of *Rolling Stone*. Maybe you saw the picture?"

"I'm sorry."

"It's okay. I have a copy. I'll get it."

"Ah . . . Mrs. Russell . . ." Norah called out, but she was already heading into one of the adjoining bedrooms. Norah couldn't do much more than raise her eyebrows at Ferdi and shrug before Gloria Russell was back. She carried a big album swollen with photographs and clippings. She sat and balanced it in her lap. She opened it unerringly to the page she wanted and waved Norah over.

"Want to see, Sergeant?" she summoned Ferdi.

They'd been married not before an altar but on a stage; not in the soft glow of candles, but in the harsh glare of theater spotlights. The wedding party wore western garb, heavy on the sequins. The happy couple looked dazed. Also a lot younger. The years had not been kind to either one, though perhaps Bo's chubby, choirboy face showed less wear and tear than hers. Probably that was because he stayed away from the booze and casual sex. That was according to Ellie Lyras. According to Lyras, when he was home, Bo Russell still sang in church on Sunday—for free.

"What do you think?" his wife asked eagerly. "Great, huh?"

In the picture, the bride looked almost the same age as the groom. Four years later, the wife looked ten years older than her husband, which was about right, Norah thought.

"Great," Norah and Ferdi murmured.

"And here, look here." Gloria Russell turned some pages and pointed. "Here's Ben. He's not crying, is he?"

"No," Norah agreed. There was no question but that Ben was enjoying himself. His face glistened with sweat. He had a glass of champagne in one hand and his arm wrapped around the bare shoulders of a nubile wedding guest. No way did he look the part of the rejected suitor.

"In spite of all the glamour, I don't suppose it's an easy life."

The sympathy was unexpected and welcome. "No, as a matter of fact, it isn't."

"Do you usually travel with the group?"

"Always. Bo wants me with him."

"And you want to be with him."

"Well, sure."

"But it's not easy living out of suitcases, rehearsing at all hours of the day and night," Norah suggested.

"Oh, I don't go to rehearsals."

"You don't?"

"I did at the beginning, but after a while it got boring. I mean, they'll repeat the same eight bars over and over and over. I can't tell any difference. It drives you crazy."

"So you weren't in the studio on the night Ben was killed?"

"No."

"Where were you?"

"In bed, asleep."

"Do you go to the concerts, the opening nights, the parties?"

"Oh, sure. That's different. That's fun. Or used to be. The thing is that lately Bo is so worn out after a show or a recording session, he doesn't want to go to parties. He just wants to come back to the suite."

"Not much fun for you."

"No, it isn't. Bo keeps telling me to go without him, but he doesn't mean it and I couldn't be comfortable alone."

"Couldn't one of the group escort you?"

"I wouldn't go with anybody else."

"Since Bo himself suggested . . ."

The door opened and the singer walked in. He was carrying a large stuffed teddy bear. He looked excited and happy. Seeing the two detectives, however, he became anxious. "Hello, Lieutenant. Sergeant. Anything new?"

"We're making progress."

Russell frowned. "Forgive me, Lieutenant, but that's not much of an answer. The thing is . . . we can't hang around here indefinitely."

"I understand that."

"So how much longer is it going to take?"

"I wish I knew."

"We're going to have to get it done," he told her. "We're going to have to cut the album and move on. We've already spent too much time and money on it. We've got other commitments."

"You've been very cooperative and we appreciate it," Norah replied. "We've just about finished taking statements from your people. There's general agreement that your brother was a womanizer. Seems he had a girl in every town, including here in New York. We'd like to talk to her, but so far no one has identified her."

"I can't help you."

"Maybe Mrs. Russell . . ."

"No." He was curt. "Why should Gloria know when nobody else does?"

"No offense, Mr. Russell, but your wife was once his girlfriend."

His face darkened. "So were a lot of others before and after. The turnover was heavy. Ben himself couldn't keep track."

"The waitress in the coffee shop," Gloria Russell blurted out. "The redhead, Helene. Try her."

Bo groaned.

"What makes you think she and your brother-in-law were involved?" Norah asked.

Her eagerness passed. "The way they looked at each other."

"That's all?"

"Oh, for God's sake, Gloria!" Bo exploded.

Under her heavy makeup, his wife flushed. "I saw her coming out of his room."

"So?"

"It was late. After one in the morning. Room service closes at midnight."

Shaking his head, Bo Russell turned away and placed the teddy bear on the sofa.

"Do you remember what day you saw the waitress coming out of Ben's room?" Norah asked.

"No."

"You're on the twelfth floor here. He was on the eighth. What were you doing down there?"

Clearly she hadn't expected to be quizzed. But she recovered quickly. "I was looking for Bo. There was an important phone call for him. He was supposed to be with Ben."

"Wouldn't it have been easier to ring the room?"

"Of course, and I did, but there was no answer. Lots of times they don't bother to answer," she explained. "If they're working and they're caught up in a new idea, I don't think they even hear the phone."

"So you went down to the eighth floor to look for your husband and you saw this waitress, Helene, come out of your brother-in-law's room. It was one a.m."

"Around that time, yes."

"You remember the time, but not the date."

"The days are pretty much the same."

Norah let the comment pass. "Did you finally locate your husband?"

"I didn't have to. He was here when I got back."

Norah addressed herself to the star. "Do you remember the occasion, Mr. Russell?"

"Afraid not. I depended on Ben for advice. I consulted him on just about everything. More often than not I went down to his room so as not to disturb Gloria. Obviously, this particular time, I didn't stay long."

"I see. How about the call? Do you remember that?"

He spread out his hands in a gesture of futility. "I get

so many calls—from the Coast, from overseas, at every hour of the day and night. I don't know which particular one this was."

"Mrs. Russell?" Norah tried once more.

"I think it was from the Coast. "Well, maybe not.""

"Thank you. If anything should occur to you . . ." She got up and so did Ferdi. "When are you scheduled to leave New York?" she asked.

"We're scheduled into Shea a week from today." He paused. "Unless they cancel us."

"And after that?"

"I'll have Herb send you a copy of the itinerary."

"Thank you." As she prepared to go, Norah's eyes rested briefly on the stuffed toy Russell had set on the sofa. "That's the most cuddly thing I've ever seen. Some child is going to be very happy."

All at once the singer relaxed. "It's for our son." He beamed.

"Oh? I thought . . . I'm sorry, I understood . . ."

Russell put his arm around his wife and hugged her. "Gloria's pregnant," he proclaimed. "We just found out."

"Well, that's wonderful. Congratulations."

"Congratulations," Ferdi echoed.

"The doctor says it's a boy. Nowadays they can tell."

"Wonderful," Norah repeated.

"We're not making a public announcement . . . under the circumstances."

"I wish you both great joy," Norah said.

But neither of the expectant parents was listening. Bo had a square jeweler's box in his hands. From it he drew a necklace of shimmering gold, which he placed around his wife's neck. The last they saw, he was fastening the clasp.

Chapter 10

"I'd say the joy is pretty much one-sided," Ferdi Arenas commented as he and Norah rode down to the lower level of the hotel.

"It's going to mean a big change in Gloria's lifestyle," Norah pointed out. "No more smoking or boozing. Whatever partying she's been doing, she's going to have to cut out. She'll have to watch her diet and get her eight hours."

"I don't suppose she'd even consider an abortion?"

"Are you kidding? Did you see the look on Bo's face when he told us his wife was pregnant?" Norah asked. She had seen it and understood. "He positively glowed. More than anything in the world Bo wants to pass on his name," she explained. "He'd just about given up hope that Gloria would conceive, when Ben's girlfriend got pregnant. He nearly went crazy when Ben talked abortion. Now Gloria's pregnant at last and it means everything to Bo. If Gloria's smart, and I think she is, she'll make every sacrifice to give him a healthy son and then, as the mother of his son, she can ask for whatever she wants."

"If he still has the money to pay for it."

Norah had no comment on that. Turning the corner, she pointed to a door at the end of the corridor. The sign above it read: "The Nook."

It was a typical hotel coffee shop, decorated to look like an English pub though no liquor was sold. At that hour there were no customers. Three waitresses stood at the back having a smoke and talking among themselves. The casher was reading a newspaper.

"Are you open?" Norah asked.

The cashier looked as if she was tempted to say no. "Have a seat."

"Is Helene on duty? We'd like to sit in her section."

They chose a booth in the area indicated by the cashier, and in due course a small, pert, rosy-cheeked young girl presented herself. The nameplate pinned to the pocket of her bright pink uniform read: "Helene."

"Ready to order?" she asked in a squeaky, teenager's voice. Pad and pencil at the ready, she went up and down on her toes while waiting. Ben liked them young all right, but Norah hadn't expected the girl would be this young.

Suddenly she realized she was very hungry. "I'll have fried eggs and Canadian bacon and whole wheat toast. And coffee. Coffee right away, please."

"The same for me," Ferdi said.

They looked across the table at each other, aware of sharing the excitement. Quelling their eagerness, they remained silent till the girl returned to set out the coffee cups, and brought the carafe.

"I understand The Earth Shakers are staying at this hotel," Norah began. The girl didn't respond. Norah tried again. "That must be thrilling."

The girl shrugged. "I'm into hip-hop. They don't do that."

"Too bad. Do you get to see much of the musicians? Do they ever come in here?"

"Sometimes. Depends. They're in and out."

The reaction was not what it should have been from a normal teenager even if she was into hip-hop and the group was not. Norah decided to be more direct.

"Terrible what happened to Ben Russell."

In the act of setting the cup in front of Norah, the waitress's hand shook and the coffee slopped over into the saucer. "I'm sorry." She took a wad of paper napkins out of the holder and used it to sop up.

"Did Ben Russell ever come in here? Did you ever wait on him?"

"Yeah, sure, a couple of times. I'll get you a fresh cup."

"No. Don't trouble." Norah's look to Ferdi said, You try.

"Was he a nice guy?" Ferdi asked.

"He was okay."

"Good tipper?"

"Yeah, he was." At that, she relaxed a little. "Most of them add the tip to the bill and put it all on a credit card. We don't see that money anytime soon. Ben put cash on the table."

"How about the other guests? How did they feel about having the group in the hotel?"

"We have a lot of people who live here permanently. They complain about the comings and goings, the parties in the rooms, the noise . . . like that. The neighborhood kids"—she grinned—"they hang out in the lobby for autographs. The regular guests don't go for that either."

Ferdi grinned too. "I hear Ben Russell was very popular with the ladies. I hear they practically threw themselves at him."

The waitress stiffened and Ferdi knew he'd gone too far.

"Are you reporters?"

"We're police officers." Norah showed her shield case.

"Both of you?" she asked, though Arenas also pulled his ID.

"I'm Lieutenant Mulcahaney and this is Sergeant Arenas. We're investigating Ben Russell's murder."

She paled. "I don't know anything about the murder."

"You're a smart girl and I don't think much gets by you," Norah said. "You waited on Ben Russell. You must have formed an opinion about him—beyond the fact that he was a good tipper."

"Well . . ."

"Obviously he liked you," Norah went on. "When he ordered from room service, he did particularly ask for you."

"Who told you that?"

"Am I wrong? After the dining room closed, he would be ordering through the coffee shop, wouldn't he? He was accustomed to having you serve him, so naturally he'd ask for you. I'm sure there are records we can check."

Helene went from pale to rosy red. "So he liked me. What's wrong with that?"

"Did you like him?"

"That's none of your business."

"It wouldn't be if he hadn't been murdered. Murder changes everything. Whether he asked for you or not doesn't really matter. You were seen coming out of his room well after one a.m. Room service closes down at midnight."

"All right, so we had sex. What about it?" She tossed her head.

"How often?"

She bit her lip, glanced at Norah and Ferdi, then lowered her eyes. "Do I have to say?"

"It would be best."

"A couple of times."

"Was one of them on the night he was killed?"

"No." She answered promptly, leaving no room for uncertainty.

"Did you see him at all that day or night?"

"No. They were rehearsing all day and I quit early. Three p.m. I wasn't feeling good. You can ask the manager. I went straight home. You can ask my boyfriend. So whoever says I came out of Ben's room that night is lying."

Gloria Russell had only said she'd seen the waitress coming out of Ben's room at one a.m., she hadn't specified the night. Helene was defending herself without having been charged.

Norah produced her notebook. "Your full name, please?"

"Helene Galinas."

"Your boyfriend's name?"

"Vinnie. Vinnie DeCicco."

"Where can we reach him?"

"Do you have to? He doesn't know about Ben."

Norah remained silent.

"Vinnie doesn't know what happened that night."

"But you do."

"I don't. I swear. I did quit early that day like I said. And I did go home. I had a date with Vinnie and I was going to cancel, but I haven't seen much of him lately and I was feeling better so . . . we had dinner and went to the movies and he brought me home around eleven. About eleven-thirty as I was getting into bed, my phone rang. It was Ben. He said the recording session had been called off. It was still early, so why didn't I come over?"

"And you got up, dressed, and went to meet him."

"He sweet-talked me into it," she protested, but there was a quiver of excitement in Helene Galinas's voice that she couldn't hide.

111

"Where do you live, Miss Galinas?"

"Sunnyside. It's just over the Queensboro Bridge."

"I know the area. Do you live alone?"

"With my parents."

"I see. So after your boyfriend brought you home and when your parents thought you were safely in your bed and asleep, you sneaked out to meet Ben Russell."

"I shouldn't have done it. I know it was wrong. I couldn't help myself."

Norah kept her attitude strictly neutral. "Then what happened?"

"Nothing. Absolutely nothing. I got here to the hotel, went up in the service elevator, and knocked at Ben's door. He didn't answer. I knocked and knocked. Nothing. I didn't know what to make of it. I tried calling on the house phone. No luck with that either. Then I thought he might have left a message for me at the desk. He had. The note said something had come up, but he'd meet me at Triumph Studios. He told me to go around to the back, that he'd leave the door on the latch for me."

Norah and Ferdi exchanged glances.

"When I got there, the door was locked. I rang the night bell, but nobody answered. I was disgusted and went home."

"We'd like to believe that, Miss Galinas," Norah said.

"It's the truth."

"This note Ben Russell left for you at the lobby desk, do you still have it?"

"No."

"How did you know it was from Ben? Did you recognize his handwriting? Had you ever seen his handwriting before?"

She shook her head. "No, except for his signature on the room service chits. Who else would have written it? Why would anybody else have written it?"

*   *   *

"Very productive," Norah commented as she and Ferdi left the Park West.

While they were inside, clouds had gathered, bringing an early darkness. Norah automatically turned uptown toward the station house. Ferdi lagged a couple of steps behind, studying the sky.

"The prediction is for heavy downpours later. Looks like earlier to me," he said.

All at once Norah remembered that this was a big night for her friend, his and Concepción's wedding anniversary. "Go home, Ferdi. I'll file the report."

"It's okay, I've got plenty of time. Our reservation isn't till eight."

"Good. Get home early and surprise Concepción." He was taking his wife to Tavern on the Green. He had been talking about it for weeks. "Don't argue, Ferdi. I want to write this up myself and I need to do it while it's fresh in my mind. So go home. Pick up a bunch of flowers and a bottle of champagne on the way."

"I will. Thanks, Norah."

"Have a good time." She waved him off.

A distant rumble of thunder warned her to get moving too. A gust of wind lashed the trees, stripping leaves, and whipped those few pedestrians still out. It blew grit into Norah's eyes. She ran the next two blocks and needed both hands to pull the door of the station house open; the wind slammed it shut behind her.

It was quiet inside the Two-oh. Norah nodded to Brownsteen, who was again holding down the desk. There wasn't much activity in the squad room either. As she came in, Nick Tedesco looked up from the sports section of the *Times*. She shook her head to indicate she didn't need him just yet, so he went back to reading. Sutphin was at his desk. He looked up, but avoided eye contact. Danny Neel was the only other person there.

"How's it going, Lieut'?"

"Not bad," she replied, absurdly grateful for the greeting.

As she entered her office and turned on the lights, the first fat drops of rain splattered across her window. Maybe it would only be a short shower and stop by the time she was ready to leave.

Having finished filling out the standard DD5, Norah began to set down a more detailed and informal account of the chain of events relating to the murder of Ben Russell. It was her habit to put everything on paper. That both cleared her mind so she could interpret what was known and made room for new information. The list was chronological, but if something out of sequence occurred she noted it anyway to make sure not to lose it. She'd been working close to an hour when her phone rang.

"Homicide. Lieutenant Mulcahaney."

Silence. But the line was open. There was somebody there.

"Hello? Who is this?"

Another wait and then a harsh voice. "You're not fit to be a mother."

"What?" Her body twitched as though an electric current had passed through.

"You've got no business adopting a child. We'll see to it you're turned down."

"We?" She seized on the pronoun. "Who's we? Who are you?"

"You don't belong in the department. Get out. Resign, or you'll wish you had."

"What are you talking about?"

But the caller had hung up.

Norah sat there with the receiver in her hand—frozen. Slowly, she put it back in the cradle. A while longer and she stood up, walked to the door, opened it, and looked out. Nothing had changed. Tedesco was still at his desk, though he had set the sports section aside and was typing. Neel was eating. Sutphin was on the phone.

It couldn't have been one of them, she thought, and was shocked that she should even consider such a thing. Surely Tedesco and Neel were loyal to her. The only one who had a grudge was Sutphin. Would he go to such lengths to retaliate because she'd identified him as having been present at the rally? How could it be Sutphin when he was right here under her eyes? Unless someone outside had made the call for him?

Her breath came in short, shallow gasps. How could she have been unaware of the antagonism around her? How could she have been so insensitive? For the first time in her career, Norah found herself the object not only of resentment but of active retaliation. She realized how easy things had been for her in the past when she'd had Joe to teach her and to smooth her way, and Jim Felix to steer the right assignments to her. She thought women had been accepted and assimilated into the department. She was wrong. By pointing her finger at Sutphin she had brought her situation to a head. So what was she going to do about it? One thing she was sure of: she didn't want the squad to split over her. For the time being, she wasn't going to say anything about the calls. But she had to get out of there. The pain in her chest was excruciating. She needed air. Without checking the weather, Norah grabbed her coat and purse and flung out the door and through the squad room.

The men looked up. Tedesco and Neel started to say something, but at the look of her waited till she was gone.

"What was that all about?" Neel asked at large.

"Search me," Tedesco replied.

Sutphin remained silent.

Friday, September 25
7:30 p.m.

The much-heralded storm had produced a brief but heavy downpour, almost tropical in its suddenness and force. Inside her office, Norah had been too preoccupied to notice. When she emerged, the rain had passed and a strong wind was clearing the clouds. An ominous rumble from the west, however, warned there was more on the way. In fact, she could see the dark turbulence forming. If she walked across the park she might get caught in the next shower. Should she risk it, or take the subway? She hesitated briefly at the subway entrance, then decided she felt like walking. Immediately, she slowed down. The pain in her chest eased; her breathing became deeper and regular. She felt calmer and began to reason.

Fifteen years ago women officers had brought a class-action suit against the N.Y.P.D. charging sex discrimination. In the interval, antagonism between men and women simmered beneath the surface. Because things had gone smoothly for her, Norah assumed it was the same for the other women. She'd heard ugly stories about how some of the women were treated, but she'd dismissed them. She realized now she'd been lucky in escaping. Now it had caught up with her, and she'd have to learn to deal with it. After all, what did they really have against her? She hadn't lied about Sutphin. He *had* been at the rally while on duty. How far would they carry the harassment? What could they do to her?

Nothing, she decided. Could they really interfere with the adoption? Of course not. What she couldn't shake off was that the caller knew about the adoption. That marked him as one of her inner circle.

Should she call Sister Beatrice in the morning and ask to see her? She could tell Sister what was going on, tell her side first. On the other hand, suppose the caller didn't really intend to contact Sister Beatrice. Wouldn't she be playing into his hands?

Following a path that skirted the lake and cut across the park from west to east, Norah approached the Bow Bridge. It was a small footbridge, its high arch spanning a narrow neck of water connecting two larger bodies, designed more for scenic effect than practicality. It was a symbol of bucolic tranquillity in the middle of Manhattan, as recognizable as the Empire State Building or the Twin Towers. Norah passed there frequently; often she sat on a bench at the water's edge and imagined herself far away from the stress of the city and The Job. She did so now without any idea of time passing, of the clouds massing overhead, of the deepening dark, till she heard the scream. It was a woman's scream of pure terror.

Where had the scream come from?

"Help!" The voice was high-pitched, shrill.

Norah made a slow turn in place. The area was favored by tourists, lovers, joggers, strollers, boaters, roller skaters in summer, ice skaters in winter, mothers with infants, teenagers. Artists set up easels and put the scene on canvas from every possible angle. Tonight there was no one. Norah was alone. The lampposts, designed to look like old-fashioned gaslights, glowed dimly. On her side of the bridge two of them were out, but on the other side, at the entrance to the Ramble, they were all lit. They should be. The Ramble was an area of twists and turns, of glades and arbors and gazebos. Ugly confrontations had taken place there. Natural beauty had been tainted. New Yorkers knew and stayed clear.

Straining to see and to hear, Norah became aware of

movement on the other side. Suddenly two figures emerged from the shrubbery. The girl was first. She wore spandex running pants and a bulky sweatshirt. Her hair was long, straight, a light brown threaded with gold in the glow of the lights. She was covered with dirt and bits of twigs and sodden leaves. Following close behind her was a tall, well-built man in black sweats. As she observed, Norah also interpreted. The girl appeared to have been attacked and brought down in a wooded area. She had managed to break loose and was making a run for it. She was on the verge of getting away when, suddenly, she pitched forward and fell. Her pursuer took a flying tackle and grabbed her ankles.

"Police officer!" Norah shouted. "Let her go. Now."

Momentarily startled, the man loosened his grip and looked around. The girl took advantage of the opportunity and scrambled to her feet. She catapulted down the path toward the western boundary of the park and disappeared around a bend.

Norah had her gun in hand. "Police officer," she called again, though with less urgency. "Freeze!"

She started to the bridge, intending to cross over, but he was back on his feet. His right hand dropped to his waist. Moonlight struck a glint off metal as he drew the gun and aimed it at Norah.

She fired first and watched in horror as he sank slowly to his knees and then toppled over.

She waited for what seemed like an interminable time for some movement, for some sign of life from the man she had just shot. Her heart pounding, the echo roaring in her ears, Norah Mulcahaney crouched low and, using the sides of the bridge for cover, crossed. He was lying on his side, face turned away from her. Blood had soaked through the sweatshirt at the shoulder. As she drew near, he moaned.

Norah stopped instantly; her grip on the gun tightened. There was no further sound, nor any movement. She broke out in a cold sweat. *At least he's alive,* she thought. *Thank God.*

She had to get help for him, but she needed someone to stay with him. The girl was long since gone, of course.

"Help!" Norah called in her turn. "Police officer needs assistance."

Her voice was lost in the darkness.

She moved closer to the wounded man and around to where they could see each other. "I'm a police officer," she told him. "I'm going to get help. Okay? I'll be right back."

His eyes were glazed. She couldn't tell whether or not he'd understood, but she couldn't afford to waste any more time. Just around the bend where the girl had gone, Norah knew, there was a public telephone. She only prayed it was working. "I'll be right back," she assured him once more, and then left.

Before turning the bend, whether by instinct or because she heard movement—she was never to be sure which—something made Norah stop and look around. What she saw astounded her. The man she'd left for near dead was on his feet once more, gun in hand, and pointing it directly at her.

She couldn't run; her legs refused to move. She couldn't call out; her voice was strangled in her throat. All she could think of was how her husband, Joe, had faced a pair of would-be rapists. He had faced them gun in hand and stopped to identify himself. But they had riddled him with bullets as he stood there. He had not gotten off a single shot. Norah raise her gun and took careful aim.

It was only when she felt the kick of her gun travel up through her arm that she knew she'd actually fired.

She couldn't see the blood spurt and spread across the victim's chest, but she saw him go down. She waited, but he didn't move. Instinct told her this time he would not get up again. Still, she approached cautiously once more to make sure. Bending down, she felt for the carotid artery. That was procedure, and procedure was all she had. But it was too late. The pulse of life was gone.

She took a long, close look. He was young, about twenty-five, and handsome. His face was narrow, nose aquiline, lips sensually full. His jogging outfit was of good quality. Not the kind of man you'd expect to be chasing a girl through the Ramble. He had a deep gash along one cheek, still fresh. Inflicted by the girl?

Norah holstered her gun and once again headed for the telephone. She called 911, made her complaint, and left it to them to do the rest, like any civilian. Then she returned to the victim and sat down on a nearby bench to wait.

The first to respond was a patrol car from the Central Park precinct. The car was manned by two officers; in the daytime most cars carried only one. The car left the main road and came down along the footpath, catching Norah in the headlights. She held up an arm to shade her eyes. It wasn't till they took a good look at her ID that they turned off the lights, leaving her temporarily blinded. It was a taste of what being on the other side was like, she thought. She told them what had happened and waited while they slowly and laboriously wrote it down in their notebooks. She could hardly contain herself.

Communications had notified the Fourth Division. Al Sutphin caught the squeal and Nicolas Tedesco came with him—extra fire power due to the involvement of a detective lieutenant. They approached from the opposite bank, but because the bridge was too narrow to accommodate the car, they got out and walked.

"Lieutenant," Tedesco began, but at the sight of her white face and the forlorn look in her eyes, he stopped. "Are you all right?"

"No," she replied bluntly.

It took Tedesco aback. In his mid-forties, somewhat overweight, his dark hair thick and showing no gray, Nick Tedesco was still good-looking. Married to his childhood sweetheart, he was a devoted family man. Family and job were the core of his life. When the rotation permitted, he never failed to be home for dinner and he expected every one of his boys to be present. He loved and was loved in return; he also expected to be obeyed. It was different at work. There he followed orders. The orders were issued by the lieutenant. He didn't question her right to give them, or her qualifications for the rank she held. He had always found her calm, confident, and in control. Deeply shocked at her present state, he looked to Sutphin for help. Al shrugged and walked away, leaving Tedesco to deal with the situation.

"No, of course not, you wouldn't be." Tedesco wanted to help, but he didn't know how. "We can get the basic facts from the uniforms and you can fill in the details in the morning. I'll get somebody to drive you home."

"No. I'd rather do it now."

"Sure. Get it over. Whatever you say, Lieutenant."

Norah took a deep breath and began. Once again she recounted the events that led to the fatal shooting. The words spilled out. Next, careful not to destroy the integrity of the scene, Norah pointed out to the two men from the Fourth and the newly arrived forensic team where the would-be mugger and the girl had emerged from the Ramble. She indicated where she'd been standing when she fired the first shot and where he had gone down. His blood on the ground verified it. She explained how she'd gone back and found him wounded but alive and then left him to call for help.

Finally she led them along the path toward the telephone. She described that feeling of danger at her back: they'd all experienced it at one time or another. She told them how she'd turned just in time to see him taking aim. Again she'd been forced to shoot first.

The lieut's account was logical and credible, Tedesco thought. He was a lot more at ease about the situation now than he had been. "Did you find any ID on him, Lieutenant?"

"I didn't look," Norah replied. In fact, after ascertaining that he was indeed dead, she had avoided further contact. "I didn't think I should be the one to search him."

"No, naturally not. Right. Well, we'll take care of it."

"Thanks."

Norah went back to sit on the bench while Tedesco and Sutphin and the crime scene specialists fanned out, doing the work in which she usually participated. Portable floodlights were turned on so that the scene and the body could be photographed. A general search ensued, with particular attention paid to the areas she had pointed out. Were they checking her story? It was routine, she reminded herself. She watched as the investigators scrutinized the shrubs along the path, looking for broken branches, for threads snagged from the girl's clothing, strands of hair. She was on the verge of getting up and going over to remind them that these would be clues to the victim, not the perp. Routine, they would remind her. Sutphin and Tedesco separated from the others and took a long, slow tour of the body.

Norah turned her head. She didn't want to watch anymore.

In due course, the morgue wagon arrived. Directly behind it, Dominick Jasper, an assistant M.E., pulled up.

He was short, unprepossessing, and at thirty-nine already balding. Neither the pencil-thin mustache nor the sparse beard added much in the way of distinction or authority. But Dominick Jasper was expert at his job; Norah had encountered him several times and could attest to it. They had worked smoothly together, with mutual esteem, so she was surprised when, after only a brief glance and nod in her direction, Jasper walked past her to where the victim lay. She wasn't accustomed to being a bystander. As she watched him confer with Tedesco and Sutphin, a cold chill passed through her. She realized she wasn't merely a bystander; she was the perpetrator. She had killed a man.

The victim had been hit twice—as she well knew. The first shot had grazed the shoulder. The second caught him full in the chest. He had lost his footing and fallen backward. After a brief examination, Jasper motioned to the detectives for help and they turned him over. Looking for exit wounds no doubt, Norah thought. After only a few moments, they eased him back to his original position. Doc Jasper got up but the detectives remained on their knees.

What am I doing watching from this distance? Norah asked herself suddenly. *What am I hiding from?* She had acted in self-defense, but she was behaving as though she were in some way culpable. It didn't matter who had caught the squeal, Tedesco or Sutphin or anybody else; she was the C.O.; she was in charge. So she would start by conferring with Doc Jasper. No need for him to worry about the time of death; she could fix it for him precisely. But before she made a move toward him, Tedesco and Sutphin approached.

"Lieutenant?" Tedesco was an uneasy spokesman. "The victim's name is George Koster. He lives on West End Avenue. He's in the jewelry business."

So it would have been normal for him to be carrying, Norah thought, nodding with satisfaction. "Good work. Most New Yorkers know enough to stay out of the Ramble," she reasoned. "The girl could have been from out of town, of course. It would be good if we could locate her. We could put out an appeal."

"First thing in the morning," Tedesco promised.

"Did you find the name of the next of kin?"

"A Mr. and Mrs. Koster. His parents probably. They live in Woodmere."

"Under the circumstances, you'd better do it," Norah decided. Usually she was the one who made the notification.

"Right, Lieutenant."

"So if we're through here, I'll come back to the squad with you and make my statement."

Tedesco swallowed. "Actually, Lieutenant, there's a problem."

"What problem?"

"We can't find the gun."

She didn't grasp the significance of what he'd said, not right away. She had turned her service revolver over to him first thing, naturally, since it was evidence. So he must be referring to the victim's gun. She gasped.

"What do you mean, you can't find it? He had a gun. It was in his hand."

"No, Lieutenant."

"All right, it fell out of his hand. When he was hit, the impact caused him to drop it. It's got to be somewhere around. Maybe under him."

"We looked."

And indeed they had.

"We looked everywhere, believe me, Lieutenant." Tedesco's eyes spoke of his distress and helplessness. "I'm sorry."

Even Al Sutphin, standing at Tedesco's shoulder, looked like he felt sorry for her.

"He had a gun," Norah repeated. "I saw it. The moonlight glinted off the barrel. I saw it clearly," she insisted.

Looking into their faces, she saw they didn't believe her.

"I'm sorry, Lieutenant." Tedesco had lost count of how many times he'd apologized. This time it was for reading the lieutenant her rights under Miranda. "I have to do it."

"Then do it. For God's sake, let's get it over." Norah kept her head high and her chin thrust forward while Tedesco, with his head down, mumbled through the familiar phrases. He seemed not to know what to do next.

It was up to her, Norah thought. "Where's your car?"

He pointed to an '89 Toyota in the small parking area at the top of Cherry Hill.

"Okay, let's move. We've got a long night ahead." She stepped out and Tedesco and Sutphin fell in behind her.

Suspects usually rode in the rear with one of the detectives. Norah opened the passenger door at the front and took her customary place beside the driver.

She was back in charge.

It was a short ride to the station house, but the news had preceded them. Somehow, everybody in the building had found a reason to be down on the main floor when Lieutenant Mulcahaney came in. She strode into the Two-oh at the head of her detectives and stopped at the desk as she always did.

"Captain Jacoby called, Lieutenant," Brownsteen told her. "He's on his way. He wants you to wait."

"Thanks, Sergeant." She nodded as though it were

the most natural thing in the world for the captain to return at that hour.

Upstairs in the squad room, Danny Neel was covering the chart. As soon as he saw her, he got to his feet. "Anything you want, Lieutenant?"

"Not right now."

"Wyler and Arenas called. They're on their way."

Simon had been contacted at his home, Norah thought; that was easy enough. And the whole squad knew Ferdi was celebrating with his wife at Tavern on the Green.

"Get hold of them and tell them there's no need for them to come. I'll see them in the morning." She was whistling in the dark, but it had the desired effect: she saw relief in Neel's face and sensed it in Tedesco and Sutphin behind her. She turned to them. "Let's start on the reports."

"Yes ma'am," they said, but neither moved.

"Write it up the way you see it. I'll do the same."

The leading edge of the next in the line of rain showers had reached midtown; the thunder broke directly overhead.

Captain Emanuel Jacoby, C.O. of the Twentieth Precinct, had reached his rank at the very top of the civil service promotion ladder by dint of hard work, dogged determination, and high marks on the written exams. The next step up, to deputy inspector, could be reached only by appointment, and Jacoby did not have the presence to impress his superiors. He had little street experience, but he was a strong administrator. Though he went strictly by the book, he acknowledged there were times when that was not possible or even desirable. He was a fair man and known to support his people. If one of them was charged with an illegality and could convince him that he or she had acted justifiably, Jacoby would stand behind the officer. He was respected for that.

Over the years, Manny Jacoby and Norah Mulcahaney had faced each other many times across a desk—his, hers, downtown in the Big Building—and had forged a bond of understanding. As C.O., he kept relatively regular hours. For him to return to the station house long after he left for the day, at a time when he should have had his swollen feet up on a stool while he watched baseball on television, was an indication of his concern for Norah.

They met in his office.

"I talked to the D.A.," he told her. "If a gun had been found on the victim or anywhere at the scene, there'd be no question that the charge would be dismissed. But as it is . . ." Jacoby raised his pudgy hands and dropped them.

"I know. I understand," Norah replied.

"He can't just ignore the absence of the gun. You'll have to be arraigned, but you'll be released on your own recognizance, of course. Then . . ."

"I'll have to appear before the grand jury."

"Not necessarily. That will depend on the determination by I.A."

She was well aware of the process. Norah had testified three times before Internal Affairs panels. In each instance, she had appeared on behalf of another officer, the defendant. This time she herself was the defendant. The point was that she knew the drill. Why was Jacoby reviewing it?

He went on. "Of course, this is a period of stress for all of us because of that rally. You're upset about having had to identify Al Sutphin on the video tape. What with the Rocker and García cases you're carrying a particularly heavy load. Then there's your own personal situation . . ."

Norah stiffened. "What about it?"

"You've applied to adopt a child. Naturally, you're anxious about whether you'll qualify."

"You want me to say I was so stressed out that I imagined George Koster had a gun? That I panicked? Overreacted?"

"It would be understandable."

"No."

"You said moonlight glinted on the barrel. It could have struck off his watch bracelet, or . . . a ring or . . ." He shrugged helplessly. "Who knows."

Norah clenched her fists at her sides to keep them from shaking. She gritted her teeth till she was sure she could speak without a quaver. "I killed a man, Captain. I didn't do it because moonlight glinted off his wristwatch."

"Did you do it because in a similar situation your husband failed to?"

She took a long time answering and then it wasn't a direct answer. "There was a gun."

Jacoby sighed. "Then what happened to it?"

"I don't know. Maybe while I was on the phone somebody came by, saw it, and took it."

"Not likely."

"But possible," Norah said. "We need to know more about Koster and about the girl. If she comes forward . . ."

"It's a long shot," Jacoby warned, and seeing that Norah was about to offer more arguments, hurried on. "We'll investigate. We won't leave one stone unturned. Trust me. But you're to stay out of it. I don't want anybody to be able to suggest you manufactured evidence."

"Manufactured!"

"We can't be too careful. So you'll stay on the job—business as usual. Which means you'll continue to head up the Rocker and García cases. That's a vote of confidence from the P.C. on down. I hope you realize that, Norah."

"I do, Captain."

"Good. I talked to Chief Felix. We expect flak from the media, but we'll handle it."

"Thank you."

"Don't thank me. As I told you, this comes from the top. You could have been suspended."

She nodded. She had half expected she would be.

It could still happen, he was on the verge of adding, but the look on her face told him she knew that too. "I suggest you keep a low profile for the next few days—get out in the field and stay away from the precinct and the media. Don't take calls at home."

His last comment shook her. Did he know about the hate calls she'd been getting? He couldn't, she decided. Should she tell him? How would Manny Jacoby react? Would he consider it an additional threat to her emotional stability?

Chapter 11

At the foot of the Queensboro Bridge, tucked behind Queens Boulevard, lay a neighborhood of modest row houses. Freshly painted, each had its own carefully tended square of garden. In fact, it was the color of the paint and the choice of flowers, which in this late September were in riotous bloom, that distinguished one house from another; otherwise, they would have been as alike as paper cutouts. Driving slowly to scan the numbers, Norah was impressed that there was not a scrap of litter anywhere—not on the sidewalks or in the gutters. No trash cans were to be seen; probably they were kept at the back till just before pickup. Something struck her as odd, however, and it took a while to figure out what. It was Saturday, a warm, sunny morning, and there were no children.

Having located the number she wanted, Norah pulled up, mounted the steps to the door, and rang. The door was opened by a squat woman with iron-gray hair and light gray eyes. She was wearing a flowered cotton housedress, ankle socks, and Reeboks.

"Mrs. DeCicco?"

"Yes?"

"I'm looking for Vincent. Is he at home?"

"What do you want him for?"

"I'm a police officer." Norah showed her ID. "I need to ask him a few questions, that's all."

"Questions? What questions? What's he done?"

"Nothing. Nothing at all, Mrs. DeCicco." Why was she so defensive? Had there been trouble with the police before? Norah wondered. Did Vinnie have a record? Maybe a juvenile record? That wouldn't be easy to trace.

"He's a good boy, Miss . . . Officer," the mother pleaded. "Actually, that's the problem. People think because he's slow, he's dumb. He's not. He's good-hearted—he believes what people tell him. People use him."

Norah was getting the picture. "I need to ask him some questions. Where can I find him?"

"At the playground. He goes every Saturday morning to play basketball. He's crazy about basketball. What questions?"

"Actually it's his girlfriend, Helene Galinas, I'm interested in."

"Oh, her." Mrs. DeCicco made no attempt to mask her dislike.

"Have they been going together long?"

"Too long." She glowered.

"Did your son have a date with her last Tuesday night?"

"He has a date with her every night unless she's working late. In that case, he goes to the hotel to pick her up and take her home. He says it's too dangerous for her to ride the subway alone at night. He works for Lilco, out on the Island? He has to leave here at six. I wake him at five. What about his sleep?"

"Can you remember anything in particular about this past Tuesday? Did Vinnie pick Helene up at the hotel?"

Mrs. DeCicco frowned. "Vinnie did mention that Helene was on day duty. He was pleased about that. He was going to call for her at home, take her out to eat and see a movie."

"Is that what he did?"

"I heard him come in after eleven, so he must have."

"Which means he'd already taken her home."

"I guess."

"She lives nearby?"

"Around the corner. Why do you want to know all these things?"

There was no reason not to tell her, Norah thought. "You know Helene works at the Park West Hotel in Manhattan. One of the guests was murdered in the early hours of Wednesday morning."

"The rock singer. I read about it. I thought he was killed in a recording studio."

"That's true," Norah admitted. The story had worked its way to the front pages. It was natural for Mrs. DeCicco to take particular interest.

"You think Helene is involved?" She was clearly intrigued.

"We're investigating anyone who may have had contact with the victim."

Mrs. DeCicco was smart enough to recognize the evasion. "Look, Miss . . . Officer . . . I don't like Helene. I guess you caught on to that. She is not a good girl. She cheats on my son. Oh yes, she does. She goes out after Vinnie brings her home. I see her." She hurried to justify the accusation. "Like I told you, she lives right around the corner on that dead-end street." Mrs. DeCicco pointed. "To get to the subway she has to pass by here. So I see her when she goes and I see her when she comes back at maybe two or three in the morning. She's been with another man. What else? But I can't tell Vinnie.

He wouldn't believe me and he'd blame me for spying on her."

"You say you observed Helene coming home in the early hours on several occasions. How did this come about? Were you waiting up?"

"The first time I saw her, it was by chance. After that, I started to watch for her. But whatever Helene did, I don't believe she's involved in a murder."

Norah formed her final questions carefully. "On this past Tuesday, after your son returned from his date with Helene, did you sit at your window and look for her to go out again?"

"Yes."

"And did you see her?"

Mrs. DeCicco took a long time to answer.

"I fell asleep," she said.

Had Mrs. DeCicco fallen asleep? Norah asked herself. Or was that a convenient way to avoid telling what she had or had not seen?

In any case, Vinnie's mother had revealed more than she'd intended. It often happened that in trying to cover one thing, a witness revealed another. In her animosity toward Helene, Mrs. DeCicco had given her son a motive for murder.

Before going to the playground, Norah took a tour of the neighborhood. She wanted to see if there was a way for Helene to get to the subway from her house without being seen by her boyfriend's mother. There was. She could go out her own back door and through her backyard, passing the rear of the DeCicco house while Mrs. DeCicco watched at the front—that is, if she knew Mrs. DeCicco was watching. She might have taken that route to evade her own parents, Norah reasoned. Over a period of time, she might have gotten careless.

On the night of her last rendezvous with Ben Russell, she was excited, eager to see him, and might well have thrown caution to the wind.

No need to wonder where the children were, Norah thought as she approached the playground. She could hear them and, turning the corner, see them. The playground was teeming with children of all ages, sizes, and colors. All of them, it seemed to her, were yelling and screaming at the top of their lungs. They were skipping rope, roller-skating, taking batting practice. Norah parked, got out, and made her way through the various groups to the basketball court, where a game was in progress.

She had no trouble picking Vinnie out; he was the only adult. He was also the tallest on the court, and though she was no expert, she could tell that he was not the most skilled. However, the way both Helene and Mrs. DeCicco had talked about Vinnie, Norah had not expected he would be so good-looking. His dark hair was slicked back from a high brow. His eyes were dark, glowing against an olive complexion. Stripped to the waist in the hot sun, his well-muscled torso glistened with sweat. She stood off to one side watching him play. Finally a break was called. The whistle was blown by an older man in red sweats with the words *Sunnyside Up* stenciled across the back. Norah approached him.

"Hello. I'm from the Twentieth Precinct in New York. Lieutenant Mulcahaney." Less intimidating than announcing she was from Homicide. Norah held out her hand. "Are you in charge here?"

"Yes ma'am." His grip was firm, his hand dry and warm. "Thomas Benson. What can I do for you?"

"I came to talk to Vinnie DeCicco," Norah replied, "but I'm confused. "He's a little old to be on the team, isn't he?"

"Certainly is." Benson grinned. "He's my assistant."

"Is that a paid position?"

"No, I'm a teacher and I get paid. Vinnie is a volunteer."

"Nice to see a young man using his time like this."

"Vinnie's a good kid."

"But . . ." Norah prompted.

"Nothing."

"Is he handicapped?"

"Do you think he is? Look at him."

"He's a fine-looking young man and he seems physically fit, but he's not all that well coordinated. Am I right?"

"He holds down a good job with Lilco," the coach pointed out.

"I understand he's engaged to a local girl, Helene Galinas."

Benson shrugged. "He thinks he is. The girl uses him, I'm afraid. One of these days he's going to have a rude awakening."

Maybe he'd had it already, Norah thought.

"I see. Well, thank you. Thanks for your help." She started toward Vinnie.

"Ah . . . miss? Lieutenant?" Benson went after her. "What do you want to talk to him about?"

"That's police business."

"I'm not so sure I should let you talk to him alone . . . without someone to look out for him."

"I don't mean him any harm, Mr. Benson. You're certainly welcome to sit in if you want. Or we could all go over to the precinct together."

"I'd feel better if his mother were present."

"You sound like his lawyer, Mr. Benson, but you're not. What are you afraid of?"

"Me? Nothing."

"All right. Look, I want to talk to Vinnie about his girlfriend. Helene Galinas is involved in a murder investigation."

Benson's face went white. Crime and violence were all around him. So far, he'd been lucky—it hadn't entered his classroom or this playground. So far, he had walked through gunfire unharmed, keeping watch over his young charges. But what could he do about this?

"As far as I can tell now, Vinnie is not involved," Norah went on. "If the situation changes, he'll be advised of his rights under the law, you can be sure of that." She hadn't intended to go this far. In fact, at this stage she wasn't sure how to handle Vinnie, but she couldn't let that show. So, without another word, she stepped around Benson and went over to the young man. He had put on a T-shirt and was sitting on a bench sipping a Pepsi. Benson made no effort to follow her.

"Mind if I sit?" Norah asked, pointing to the seat beside Vinnie.

"Why not?" He smiled at her.

A good boy, a good kid, he'd been called. "Endearing" sprang to Norah's mind. "My name is Norah Mulcahaney. I'm a police officer," she told him, and offered her hand.

He took it without hesitation and met her look squarely. "I never met a lady policeman before. I've seen them on television."

"You're Vinnie DeCicco, right?"

"Right. How do you know my name?"

He was neither worried nor disturbed. Curious—he was curious. "Helene told me. Your girlfriend."

He smiled that nice smile. "We're engaged."

"You've been engaged for a long time."

He sighed lightly. "Mama doesn't like Helene. Mama's been a widow for ten years. Even though it's my money that keeps the house going, she's used to running things. If I got married and brought my wife home, my wife would be the boss. She'd take over. If I got married and moved out, then Mama would be alone. I guess she's not going to like anybody I choose."

Impeccable reasoning, Norah thought. "I understand you and Helene had a date last Tuesday."

"Yes. We ate at the Grotto. It's a ways up Queens Boulevard. It's nice. They make terrific pasta. Then we went to the movies. We saw *The Last of the Mohicans*. It was playing at the Midway. Then I took her home. She invited me in for coffee. It was about ten-thirty."

Clear, precise, and forthcoming. Norah wished all witnesses would respond like this. "What time did you get back to your house?"

"Like I said, Helene invited me in for coffee. Her dad was waiting up for her, so I didn't stay but about twenty minutes. I guess I was home by eleven. Mama was still up."

Norah wondered if it had occurred to his mother or to her parents that the young people could rent a room. "And then what happened?"

For the first time, he hesitated. "I went to bed."

She'd been prepared to go on to something else, but she caught something in his tone. "Is that the truth, Vinnie?"

Reluctantly, he met her gaze. "No ma'am. I went up to bed but I couldn't sleep. As soon as Mama went to her room and turned out her light, I got dressed and went out."

"Where did you go?"

"I went to New York to talk to Mr. Russell."

"Why?"

"To tell him to leave Helene alone. He was bothering her. She told me. He wouldn't leave her alone. He wouldn't take no for an answer. He said if she wasn't nice to him, he'd complain about her to the manager and get her fired."

Plainly, Helene Galinas had jumped in with her version of the affair, and being what he was, Vinnie believed it. But what had prompted Helene to speak?

"So you went to talk to Ben Russell."

"Yes ma'am."

"Why on that particular night?"

"Like I said, I couldn't sleep."

"Why not? What was bothering you?"

He shook his head.

"What did you think was going on between Helene and Ben Russell?" As soon as she'd spoken, Norah realized he wouldn't answer the question phrased that way. "What made you think anything was going on?"

"It happened last week. Helene was working nights. I went to pick her up like always and they told me she was delivering one last order to Mr. Russell's room and then she'd be through. I waited around at the back but she didn't come. So I went up to the eighth floor, and I saw her come out of his room. She was all red in the face and her blouse wasn't buttoned right." Vinnie flushed with embarrassment, indignation, and pain. "When she saw me, she started to cry. I wanted to bust into his room right then and have it out with him, but she wouldn't let me. She promised to stay away from him. She promised it would never happen again."

But it had and he knew it, Norah thought, suppressing a sigh. He cared for her and he could sense it had happened again. "You couldn't sleep," she recapped. "So what did you do?"

"I called Helene."

"Why?"

"Just to hear her voice."

Just to make sure she was home and in her bed, Norah thought. "Weren't you afraid to wake her parents?"

"She has her own phone in her room."

"All right. Go on."

"She didn't answer."

"So you went looking for her."

"I went to talk to Mr. Russell. I was going to warn him off."

Confronted by that simple but dogged righteousness, Russell couldn't have gotten rid of him easily. "What happened?"

"He wasn't there."

"Did you ask for him at the desk?"

"No. I didn't think he'd see me. I went straight up to his room. I knocked and there was no answer."

"What time was it?"

"I'm not sure. I wasn't thinking about the time. I guess it was after midnight."

About the time Helene got there. With the two of them wandering around the halls, it was a wonder they hadn't run into each other. "What did you do then?"

"I waited. I sat on the stairs and waited for Mr. Russell to come back."

He said it as though it were the most natural thing in the world. "I take it that from where you sat you had a clear view of the door of Mr. Russell's room?"

"Oh, sure."

"And how long did you wait?"

"Till four. I go to work at six. Mama wakes me at five. I didn't want her to find me gone and see that my bed hadn't been slept in."

According to Herb Cranston, he had called Ben's room right after speaking to Bo at 3:45 a.m., and Ben was there. By 4:30 at the latest, he was dead in the isolation booth.

"Is it possible that Mr. Russell could have left the room without your seeing him?"

"No ma'am."

"You might have been momentarily distracted. Had to go to the bathroom? Dozed off?"

"No ma'am. Nobody went in or out of that room while I watched."

Saturday, September 26
11:00 a.m.

DEADLY FIRE
POLICE OFFICER INTERRUPTS MUGGING
KILLS SUSPECT

The headlines jumped off the page at Norah as she passed the corner newsstand. Anytime a cop shot a civilian it was news. When the encounter resulted in a fatality, the cop was on the spot. He would not get the benefit of the doubt, not these days. The custom now was to put the cop under close scrutiny, examine his actions and motives while finding excuses for the victim. In this instance, there was an added fillip—the officer was a woman. She bought a copy of the paper and stepped to one side to read it.

WOMAN OFFICER FIRES TWICE
CLAIMS SHE SHOT IN SELF-DEFENSE

An eerie photograph of the scene took up the top quarter of the page. It showed the path as it curved along the lakeshore, with the water on one side and the heavy growth of the Ramble on the other. Within the dim pool of light cast by the imitation gaslight lay the body of the man Norah had shot. The reader was advised to turn to page 3.

> Detective Lieutenant Norah Mulcahaney, commander of the Fourth Homicide Division, told investigating detectives at the scene of the Central Park killing that the alleged mugger had her under the gun. It was her life or his. She fired twice. Having missed the first time, she couldn't afford to give him a second chance.

Norah gasped. She felt as though she'd been punched in the stomach. That wasn't at all what she'd said. Of course, it wasn't a direct quote. The columnist, known for his antipolice stance, was taking care not to quote anyone directly; but neither was he making up his account out of whole cloth. From whom had he drawn the inference? Not from one of her people—not Nick Tedesco, not even Al Sutphin. Nick was both too loyal and too smart to give a reporter that kind of opening. And Sutphin? He wasn't stupid either. If he was the one, he'd done it on purpose. They'd had their differences, but Norah couldn't believe he'd go to such lengths to get even. Probably the comment was based on nothing more than a careless remark by one of the uniforms or one of the technical crew.

The account continued:

> According to Lt. Mulcahaney, she was walking through the park passing below the Belvedere Tower and heading east when she heard a woman scream for help. She saw two people emerge from the Ramble—a man chasing a woman. The woman stumbled and fell. He threw himself on her. Lt. Mulcahaney called out, identified herself as a police officer, and

ordered him to release the woman. In that moment, distracted, the alleged mugger did let go and the woman fled.

Lt. Mulcahaney drew her gun and advanced with the intention of placing the suspect under arrest. Instead of submitting, he pulled a gun of his own. She ordered him to drop it, but he raised it and took aim. She fired first and he went down.

Seeing that she had hit him, Lt. Mulcahaney ran over to him to gauge the extent of the injury. He appeared not to be severely hurt, so she told him to lie still while she went to the emergency phone to get help. Looking back to check on him, she saw that he was once more on his feet with his gun raised. She had no choice but to shoot a second time.

The account was not openly critical, Norah thought. Then suddenly, with a terrible sinking sensation, she realized the writer had caught something everyone else, including herself, had missed.

After having shot the alleged mugger the first time, Lt. Mulcahaney left him without having searched him for his weapon.

How could she have overlooked that? Norah asked herself. It was basic, logical, routine. How many times had she done it in the past? If she had disarmed Koster, the incident would have ended right then and he would still be alive. She scanned the other, briefer account on the same page:

ALLEGED MUGGER CARRIED NO WEAPON
No gun was found on the body of the man Detective Lieutenant Norah Mulcahaney, head of Fourth Homicide, shot in Central Park last night. Lt. Mulcahaney stated that the victim twice threatened her

with a gun and she shot him in self-defense, yet no gun was found on him. The grounds in the immediate vicinity were searched, but no weapon turned up. Lt. Mulcahaney was not available for comment.
Internal Affairs has entered the case.

Both accounts gave Koster's name and address and mentioned that he was in the jewelry business, but failed to point out that he was in the habit of carrying large sums of money and valuable gems and that he was licensed to carry a gun. That would have been a point in Norah's favor.

Chapter 12

Norah went home. As she approached her building, she noticed two men sitting in a car parked directly across the street. Could they be I.A.? If they were, they would have been out of the car by now, flanking her, reading her her rights. If she was wanted for interrogation, a simple call ordering her to appear at a time and place of their choosing would have been enough.

Were they reporters? Reporters didn't come in pairs.

Maybe they had nothing to do with her. After all, the whole world did not revolve around her, she thought. Nevertheless, she decided to go around the block and enter the building through the service door.

Once in her apartment, Norah went directly to the living room window. They were still down there, still stolidly sitting and making no effort to justify their presence. Let them sit there all day! She turned away, and as she did so, her phone rang. Captain Jacoby had advised her not to answer but rather to let the machine record the message. It was programmed to kick in after the fourth ring. She waited.

"You shot down an unarmed man. You committed murder." The voice was harsh, throbbing with hate. "You're not going to get away with it."

Norah felt herself grow hot.

"The brass isn't going to cover for you forever. You're not teacher's pet anymore. Resign. Get out before you're thrown out."

Norah pressed the stop button and picked up the receiver. "Who is this?"

"You can't hide forever. You can't sneak into your house through the back door forever. You committed murder and you're not going to get away with it."

The line went dead. For a long moment Norah stood with the receiver in her hand; then she put it down and rushed to the window again. The two men in the car were still there. They were looking up in her direction. The one in the passenger seat waved and his partner turned on the ignition. They drove away.

Cops! Norah thought. My God, cops! She hadn't recognized either one, but she was now absolutely positive that's who they were. The fact that she didn't know them made it worse. It meant the hate was spreading. When other women in the department had recounted similar experiences, she'd thought they exaggerated. She knew better now.

What could she do about it?

The phone rang again and this time Norah snatched it right up. "Yes?" she snapped.

"It's Ferdi."

"Oh. I'm sorry. I thought . . . Never mind. What's up?"

"A couple of things. To start, Wyler's in the hospital."

"No! What happened? Is he all right?'

"Appendicitis. He's been having abdominal pain for some time and putting off seeing a doctor. In the night it got real bad, so he took himself to the emergency room. Just in time before the appendix burst."

"Is he going to be all right?"

"The doctor says yes, but he's going to be laid up for a while."

"As long as he's okay." Norah took a deep breath. "What else?"

"Tedesco talked to some of Koster's associates in the jewelry district. Koster was known to carry his piece regularly whether he had jewels or large sums of cash on him or not. Most of the dealers do. They're prime targets."

"But would he have been likely to carry it while jogging in the park?"

"You saw the gun," Ferdi reminded her gently.

"I'm beginning to wonder."

"Don't. Don't let yourself be shaken. What we need to do is find the woman Koster was after. We have to get her story. Simon was going to put out an appeal for her to come forward."

Wyler was on the Rocker case, so this was something he was doing on his own time, Norah realized.

"I told Al I'd take over for Simon if he wants," Ferdi continued. "But he says he and Tedesco can handle it."

Like Wyler, Ferdi was offering to work on his own. Norah wasn't surprised, but she was deeply grateful and didn't quite know how to express it.

"The thing is . . . I'm not comfortable with that," Ferdi confided. "Al's heart isn't in this case. He still resents your ID'ing him on the video. A lot of the men are on his side."

Men from the Fourth? Norah was afraid to ask. "I've been getting some nasty phone calls," she admitted. It was a relief to talk about it.

Ferdi groaned. "Damn. That's not right. Maybe . . . we could assign a policewoman to stay with you."

"Don't be ridiculous." Norah was dismayed and dis-heartened that he took it for granted cops had made those calls. She managed a laugh. "*I'm* a policewoman, remember?"

"You're the best, but you should have someone with you. I could come over."

"No. Absolutely not. Thanks, Ferdi, I appreciate it, but I'm okay." Then she couldn't help adding, "As long as the media doesn't blow it all up."

"They won't," Ferdi assured her. "If you change your mind and decide you do want company, I'm available."

"Thanks for everything, Ferdi."

His call had made her feel better and worse at the same time. It was evident that for now the media were holding off taking sides. If the I.A. investigation con-cluded that she'd had no justification for shooting Kos-ter, she would be charged, indicted, and go to trial. In that case, nobody, not even the P.C., could do anything for her. Manny Jacoby had ordered her not to take a hand in trying to clear herself, to let Sutphin and Te-desco and the squad conduct the investigation. She was wary of Sutphin, as evidently Ferdi was, but she believed Tedesco and the others would keep an eye on him. She'd lost Wyler, but the numbers were still in her favor. She itched to get out and help herself. The brass wanted her on the Rocker case. If she could solve that, it might be the best way to strengthen her credibility.

Norah changed into black slacks and a black-and-white-striped shirt, and put on house slippers. She fixed herself a cup of instant coffee and took it over to her desk. She slipped a blank sheet of paper into the type-writer and stared at it. Unfortunately, the Rocker case folder was at the office. But she could write up the recent interrogations, get the facts and the impressions on paper while they were still fresh.

As she worked, Norah was surprised at how much

ground she and Ferdi had covered, beginning with the interview of Ellie Lyras, the talent agent. After her, they'd talked to Herb Cranston, Bo's manager; then his wife, Gloria, and Bo himself; also Watts and Dubois. They'd traced Ben's latest girlfriend, Helene Galinas, and her boyfriend, Vinnie DeCicco.

It was too soon to expect a report on Bo's financial situation from Julie Ochs. He'd been working with Wyler, and now that Simon was laid up, Ochs might need help. Norah called the squad; he wasn't on duty. She called John Jay College; he'd been there and left. Home was the last place she expected to find him, but she tried.

"Hi, Lieutenant!"

Julius Ochs was always cheerful. He accepted all assignments with enthusiasm. Originally he had wanted to be a lawyer, but his father's death and the ensuing home obligations put the lengthy and expensive schooling out of reach. He decided on police work. He never let anyone know it was second choice, and in time he forgot that he'd ever had other aspirations. If he'd thought about it, he would have been surprised to discover that the job he was in was the job he wanted more than any other.

"How are you, Lieutenant?" The moment he said it, he winced.

Nevertheless, Norah gave him a straight answer. "Not so bad, considering the circumstances."

"Yeah, the press is being real rough on you. That guy in the *News,* what's his name? Ed Colin. He went too far." Ochs was an avid reader. He kept the entire squad informed of events and editorial comment.

"I missed that one."

"Hot air, Lieutenant. He says you panicked when you shot Koster. He also said you'd never go to trial."

"I hope he's right on that." The dogs were out, Norah thought. "What else?"

Ochs was uncomfortable—Norah could sense it. "Let's have it, Julie."

"He said women are not only physically but emotionally unfit to be police officers. But hey, he's been saying that for years."

"What's the rest of it? Come on, I can go out and buy a paper."

Ochs sighed. "He said you should be suspended pending a thorough investigation. At the very least, you should be off the Rocker case."

She had expected that cry to rise but not so soon. "Lucky for me Chief Deland doesn't feel like that. So that brings me to the reason for my call. Have you turned up anything on Bo Russell's financial situation?"

"He's hurting, I can tell you that much. Cranston's being very cooperative. He's opened the books on The Earth Shakers and also on Bo's personal income to us, and they appear in order."

"Any payments to a Miss Daisy Barth?"

"I thought you'd ask." She could hear the smile in his voice. "I've made a list. I think it will tell you what you want to know."

"Good. Can you drop it off? At my house, Julie."

"Sure."

"You know Simon's in the hospital? Can you manage on your own?"

"No problem. All the banking goes through a local branch in Bethlehem. I've filed to examine the records. I expect the okay to come through anytime, but I have to wait till it does."

"I'm going there myself. I'll look into it."

Till that moment, Norah hadn't considered the trip.

When she hung up on Ochs, Norah contacted the captain.

"I want to go to Bethlehem, Pennsylvania, to talk to

a woman called Daisy Barth," she told him. "About six months ago she gave birth to a child. The father was Ben Russell. Bo paid her medical expenses and an allowance."

"What do you expect to learn from her?"

"She was intimately involved with the brothers."

"And this is a good time for you to get out of town," Jacoby commented.

"If it's going to cause a problem, Captain . . ."

"You have a legitimate need to talk to this woman, right?"

"Yes, Captain."

"Then get moving."

Sunday, September 27
7:00 a.m.

Norah got an early start the next morning. The sun was bright, the sky blue with puffs of white clouds. Traffic was light on the interstate. Crossing into Pennsylvania near Stroudsburg, she took to the back roads. She was familiar with the area around the Delaware Water Gap. When she was a little girl, her father used to rent a cabin in the Poconos for two weeks every summer. There, along with her two older brothers, Norah hiked, swam in the quiet pools, and fished. Good memories abounded and were revived. She reached Bethlehem relaxed and optimistic, only to discover that Daisy Barth and her father were gone.

They were no longer at the address Julius Ochs had given her. According to the neighbors, they had moved out around the time Daisy was due to give birth. The neighbors gossiped freely about what they called Daisy's "shame," but they didn't know much. They had no idea where Daisy and her father had gone, though they thought they knew why. Tom Barth was a religious man. His wife died giving birth to Daisy and he had raised her all alone. He held himself responsible for what had happened. He shared in her disgrace. It was the consensus that Tom Barth decided to take his daughter away to a place where no one would know she was having a baby out of wedlock, where she could start a new life without embarrassment for herself and without branding her child a bastard. Barth was known to be reserved, to keep to himself, so it was no surprise he didn't tell anyone where he was taking Daisy. In fact, he had slipped away in the night, so it was several days before anyone even noticed he and Daisy were gone.

Norah was annoyed and frustrated. Cranston must have given Ochs the wrong address. It was his responsibility to send Daisy the money to keep her and the baby; he had to know they'd moved. Why hadn't he told Julie? Was it an oversight, or had he done it on purpose?

It was Sunday, so there was no possibility of getting a forwarding address from the post office. The banks were closed too. What should she do? Call New York and have Ochs get hold of Cranston and get the right address? In the meantime, while she waited . . . While she waited she could talk to Daisy's doctor. There weren't that many doctors in town.

Emil Landsburgh was not pleased to be interrupted in the middle of his Sunday dinner. He mellowed somewhat when he learned who Norah was and what she wanted.

Daisy Barth, he told her, was about a month from term when she disappeared. "Disappeared" was the way he characterized it. Daisy never mentioned she was planning to go away; she just didn't show up for her regular appointment. She hadn't been having an easy pregnancy, so he was concerned. He called her home, but her telephone was disconnected. He didn't know what else to do. What else could he have done?

Nothing, Norah assured him. She asked him for the names of the local hospitals. Maybe Daisy had gone to one of them when her time came.

Landsburgh was offended. Was Lieutenant Mulcahaney suggesting that Daisy Barth was not satisfied with the care he was providing?

Not at all, Norah hastened to assure him. She was floundering, she confessed. Nevertheless, it took a while to placate the doctor. Finally he calmed down enough to ask Norah to be sure to let him know if she was able to trace Ms. Barth through another hospital than the one he was affiliated with.

But that turned out to be a dead end too. Norah could find no record of Daisy's having been admitted elsewhere either under her own name or under an assumed name.

What other clue to her and her father's whereabouts could there be? Norah sat in her car and reviewed what little she knew. It was evident Barth didn't want to be found. According to Norah's information, Daisy, like everyone else, had been employed by the mill. Likely her father had too. Would he be retired by now? If so, he would be getting a pension. Regardless of how much money was coming in from Bo Russell, Barth would not be in a position to give that up, and the company had to know where to send it. No matter what day it was, the great fires were never extinguished, Norah thought; the mill never shut down. Someone, a supervisor or manager, had to be on the premises.

Norah was given an address in the vicinity of the Water Gap. She headed back the way she had come.

Sunday, September 27
8:00 p.m.

The house was tucked between the hills on the Pennsylvania side. It was part of a lonely cluster of a dozen similar frame houses, each needing varied repairs and a fresh coat of paint. They were serviced by a general store and a gas station consisting of a single pump, a hydraulic lift, and a work shed. By the time Norah arrived, it was dark and the lights were few and dim. There was a number on the mailbox, but no name. A small pickup truck was parked in a rutted driveway at the side. Norah walked up the path that cut through an unmowed front yard to a sagging porch, and rang the bell. Its timbre was tinny but reverberated in the mountain stillness. Norah didn't ring again; a light was on at the back and this wasn't the kind of place where people left a light on when they weren't home. She waited and after a while heard footsteps. The inner door was opened.

A white-haired man in a thick flannel work shirt and pipe-stem jeans stood on the threshold with the screen door between them. He was tall, but he held himself hunched forward, so it was not possible to gauge his height. The skin was loose on his frame, suggesting he had recently lost weight. His narrow face was fretted with dry lines.

"Mr. Barth?"

"Who are you?"

Norah opened her shield case and held it slanted to get some of the dim light on it. He pulled a pair of glasses from his shirt pocket, and even wearing them, had to bend down to see.

"You're a detective and you come from New York?"

"That's right. May I come in?"

His thin lips pressed into a tight line. "I suppose so." He stepped to one side.

The room was small and dreary. Everything in it sagged, including its spirit. The furniture was an assortment of discards. There were a few solid maple pieces, out of style. The upholstery was lumpy and worn. Faded rugs were strewn over washed-out floorboards. Did these things belong to the Barths, and had they cared enough about them to haul them away in the night? They looked like what might come with a summer rental, though this was not an area of summer rentals. Only the sewing machine in the corner was new. Norah shivered. Though the days of late September were warm and mellow, at night it got cold, especially here in the hills. The heat wasn't turned on.

"What do you want?" Tom Barth asked.

Whatever Bo Russell was paying the mother of his brother's child, it wasn't keeping her in luxury, Norah thought. "I'd like to speak to your daughter."

"What about?"

It had been a long, frustrating day. Norah was tired and not in the mood for verbal fencing. "Ben Russell's murder," she answered bluntly, and at Barth's blank look added, "Don't you get the papers here, Mr. Barth?"

"I don't read the entertainment section."

"Murder is front-page stuff, Mr. Barth."

"When did it happen?"

"This past Wednesday. He was shot."

"Who did it?"

He was asking when he should have been answering. Walking over to the most solid-looking of the chairs and without being invited, Norah sat. "I thought you might have some idea."

"No. I almost killed him myself when I found out what he had done to my Daisy, but the Lord stayed my hand."

"How long have you and Daisy been living here?"

"It's going on to eight months."

"Why did you come here?"

"We wanted to be in a place where people didn't know Daisy's history and where she could raise her child in a normal way, where he wouldn't have the shame of being illegitimate."

Prompt, responsive, but not a complete reply, Norah thought. Any big city would have fulfilled those requirements. Why choose this backwater?

"May I speak to Daisy?" she asked again.

"She's upstairs, resting. She hasn't been well. This news could be very upsetting."

"She doesn't know?"

Shadows filled the doorway at the far end of the room.

"What news, Pa?" From their depths, Daisy Barth spoke in a thin, tired voice.

She was spectral. Her skin was so white it was closer to blue; her lips were bloodless; her dark hair hung in dank strands. Her garments—a satin nightgown and robe that had been pink long ago—floated around her like a ghostly aura. She was an apparition, and Norah would not have been surprised to see right through her.

"What don't I know?" she asked Norah.

Norah got up. "I'm from the New York Police Department, Miss Barth. I'm investigating the death of Ben Russell."

Daisy Barth raised a thin, blue-veined hand to cover her eyes and swayed. Instantly, her father was at her side to steady her, and with a tenderness Norah would not earlier have thought him capable of, he led her to the sofa and lowered her into it. Standing slightly behind her, he looked over her head to Norah as if to say, *See, I told you.*

"I had a dream," Daisy Barth whispered, so low Norah had to bend forward to hear. "I had a dream someone tried to kill him. I wanted to warn him, but Pa wouldn't let me. Pa doesn't believe in my dreams."

Tom Barth groaned. His expression changed from tenderness to anguish.

"In this dream, could you see who it was that tried to kill Ben Russell?" Norah asked.

"No, not in that one. Maybe I will in the next."

"Do you have these dreams often?" Norah was very gentle.

"Oh yes. All the time. Sometimes they're so real it's like they were actually happening. It's scary."

"It must be," Norah agreed.

"She takes medication," Barth whispered.

Norah nodded. "Is the baby all right?"

Though they were keeping their voices low, Daisy heard and burst into tears.

"He's a fine, healthy child, thank God," Barth said in a normal tone. "She worries they'll try to take him away from her."

Of course, Norah thought. That was why Barth had chosen to come to the backwater—not merely to be free of gossip, but to be out of reach of the Russells. But now that Bo was expecting a child of his own, he'd lose interest in his brother's son. She walked over to the young mother. "Don't be upset. You have nothing to worry about." She held out her hand. "I won't trouble you any further. Good luck."

Barth escorted her to the door. "Are you going straight back to the city?"

"Yes."

"I'm sorry I can't offer to put you up for the night. We just don't have the space."

"That's all right, I'd just as soon get back. I don't suppose there'll be much traffic at this hour."

He went with her to her car, made sure she knew how to get to the highway, then watched as she drove off.

Norah had meant it when she told Tom Barth she intended to go back to New York, but as she drove, she reviewed what had transpired between her and the Barths. Something was wrong in that house. The pieces of the puzzle appeared to fit, but the picture they formed was distorted. She had reached the highway and was about to set cruising speed when she recalled the banking matter she'd intended to check. Turning off at the nearest exit, she headed back toward Stroudsburg, and pulled into the first motel that advertised a vacancy.

She was given a plain, clean, but musty room. She opened the window wide to clear both the room and her head. She slept deeply.

Monday, September 28
8:00 a.m.

It was the best night's sleep Norah had had in a long time. She got up, showered, and dressed. Last night she'd noticed a diner down the road. She left her car and walked there. After a good, hearty breakfast, she took a leisurely stroll along a country road, following the distant sound of trickling water to discover a spring which fed a rivulet that became a pond. The day was on its way to being hot, but it was still early, not yet nine. She couldn't resist sitting on a sun-warmed rock and taking off her shoes and socks to dangle her feet in the clear, cool water. The chill of it passed through her whole body, recharging her energies while the music of a small cascade soothed her mind. She didn't know how long she sat there, but she suddenly knew why she hadn't gone back to the city last night and it had nothing to do with the bank. She'd wondered why Tom Barth had chosen to come to live in this out-of-the-way, lonely crossroads. He and his daughter were hiding out. But why?

Taking a clean handkerchief from her purse, Norah dried her feet as best she could, put on her anklets and her shoes, and went back to the motel. She paid her bill and picked up her car. Once again she headed for the Barth place. The small clues that had bothered her before, each one individually not amounting to much, now imparted a strong sense of urgency taken together. She increased her speed, driving as fast as she dared along the narrow, twisting roads, afraid of slipping off the crumbling shoulder or meeting an oncoming car head-on. Arriving safely at her destination, she breathed a sigh of relief.

Last night the cluster of homes, too small to have a name, had seemed abandoned and forlorn. In the morning sunshine, the settlement bustled with activity. The door of the general store was wide open; a steady stream of housewives passed in and out. At the gas station, a young mechanic in overalls tinkered with a vintage Packard. Norah slowed to a crawl, watching the women step off their porches and hang out the wash: apparently electric washers and dryers were a luxury. The women looked up as she passed, but didn't appear interested.

There was no activity at the Barth place. The silence of the night before prevailed and hung over the ramshackle house like a smothering cloud. Noticing the pickup truck was gone, Norah felt a quickening heartbeat. Had they run away again? Surely not. She pulled over and cut the engine. Then, in the stillness, she heard a soft, steady hum. She got out, went up the path, and put her ear to the door. The hum was more pronounced. She pressed the bell. Immediately, the sound stopped.

No one came.

After a while the hum started again. And suddenly Norah knew what it was. She pressed the bell hard and held it for several moments. She was about to do it again, when she heard the click of the lock and the inner door opened.

"I'm sorry, I couldn't hear the bell over the machine," Daisy Barth apologized. She was wearing a western-style skirt that reached down to her ankles and bunched around her waist. The scoop-necked blouse fell off one shoulder. The entire outfit was too big for her. "I was just doing the ruching—" She broke off. "I'm sorry. I thought you were Mrs. Forsythe. I'm just finishing her dress to wear to the christening."

"I'm sure it's beautiful," Norah said. "May I see it?"

"If you want."

Daisy Barth flushed, and the high color became her.

She led the way to the sewing machine, which was at the back near the window. The mound of beige silk caught the light and shimmered. She held the dress up for Norah to see. It had too many ruffles for Norah's taste, but the workmanship was exquisite.

"Your work is marvelous."

"Thank you." Daisy almost looked happy.

"And these . . ." Norah went over to a side table on which infant apparel—shorts, shirts, pajamas—was stacked. "These are adorable. I bet your baby is the best dressed anywhere around."

Daisy flushed deeper. "I like to sew."

A baby in the house meant plenty of laundering,

Norah thought. In this place, it would mean clothes out on the line to dry. There were none.

"He's certainly quiet, isn't he? I don't hear a sound out of him. I didn't hear him last night either."

"He's a good baby."

Except for a pile of clothes, there was no indication of a baby.

"Where is he, Daisy? What happened to the baby?"

"Nothing happened to him. He's sleeping. He was sleeping last night."

Norah shook her head. "Where's the baby?" she asked, gently but firmly.

The tears welled up in Daisy Barth's pale blue eyes and coursed down her cheeks. "I lost him."

Norah sighed. "You had a miscarriage."

"The doctor told me I should get a lot of rest. I did a little sewing, that's all. I couldn't stay in bed all day . . ." She pleaded for Norah's understanding.

So there *was* no baby, Norah thought. Without a baby, there was no reason for Bo Russell to pay Daisy Barth. How long did Tom Barth think he could continue to collect support money for a child that didn't exist? How long could they keep up the pretense?

Norah put her arm around the sobbing girl.

Neither one of them heard Tom Barth come in.

"She can't have any more children, ever," he announced. "She's damaged goods. Who would want her?"

Thin but sinewy, he seemed to shrivel further before Norah's eyes, his physical strength oozing out along with the remnants of hope.

"The money's for Daisy. I fixed it with the post office to hold it till I pick it up, but I don't use it. We live on my pension," Barth explained. "What Bo Russell sends goes right into a trust fund for Daisy so that she'll be taken care of after I'm gone. She's not able to look out for herself."

Noting Norah's skepticism, he went on. "You'd have to see her for a while. She wanders in and out of a fantasy world where there's a little boy in a crib in the back room. She sews for him and cooks for him and she's happy. When we have to get rid of the food, when she has to face the reality that there is no child, she gets hysterical."

"I'm so sorry," Norah said. "Maybe if you explained to Mr. Russell . . ."

"I don't think so. It doesn't matter anymore. With Ben dead, he won't continue the payments."

Chapter 13

Monday, September 28
8:00 p.m.

On her return to the city, Norah was confronted by a
new set of headlines.

VICTIM OF INTENDED RAPE
COMES FORWARD
CONFIRMS SHE WAS ATTACKED BY MUGGER,
BUT DID NOT SEE GUN

MYSTERY OF MISSING GUN DEEPENS

Jocelyn Warran of West 96th Street, Manhattan, revealed she was the woman attacked in Central Park
on the night of September 25. She was taking her
customary evening jog alone because the friend who
usually ran with her had to work late.

She entered the park at East 67th Street and
headed west, following her usual route to the Boathouse. During the summer and well into the fall,
there is a lot of activity there, but the forecast had
been for heavy showers and the area was deserted.
As Ms. Warran turned onto the lake path, a man
stepped out from behind the lavatories and blocked
her. She tried to get by, but he wouldn't let her pass.

Frightened, she turned and ran in the opposite direction. With water on one side and a high, chain-link fence on the other, she had no choice but to follow the path leading straight up into the heavily wooded area known as the Ramble. Once there, she was unable to find her way out. The poorly lit, maze-like paths have been the scene for violence in the past. Plunging through the underbrush, close to the edge of the dense shrubbery and on the verge of escaping, her foot caught on a root and she fell. In a headlong tackle, the man grabbed her by the ankles. At that moment a woman, later identified as Detective Lieutenant Mulcahaney, shouted to the mugger to let her go. Distracted, he loosened his hold and Ms. Warran fled. She admits hearing shots, but was too frightened to take the time to look back.

It was much too general. Was that because whoever had interrogated Ms. Warran, probably Al Sutphin, hadn't probed deeply enough? Or were the details being purposely kept from the public?

Norah called Captain Jacoby.

"You're back. I didn't expect you so soon. How'd it go?"

"I think we can eliminate the Barths."

Jacoby took a long, deep breath. "That's the way it goes. I suppose you've seen the latest editions?"

"Yes sir, that's why I called. I'd like to talk to Ms. Warran myself."

"What is it you're not satisfied with?"

"I don't think the interrogation was thorough enough. Al Sutphin is a good investigator, but . . ."

"If you're going to say he's biased, forget it. He didn't conduct the interrogation. I.A. did."

Ouch! Norah winced.

"They also tossed Koster's home and office."

Norah held her breath.

"Nothing." Manny Jacoby answered the question she was afraid to ask. "No gun."

Thank God. A point in her favor. As long as the gun was missing, her claim that Koster had threatened her with it in the park couldn't be disproved. Should the gun turn up among his possessions elsewhere, she was finished.

"I need to talk to Ms. Warran, Captain. I've got a lot at stake here, and not just my job and my reputation. You know that I'm trying to adopt and I'm being investigated by the board at the Foundling Hospital. It's tough enough applying as a single parent, but if they think I shot a man down without good and sufficient reason, they'll conclude I'm unstable and not fit to adopt. This means everything to me, Captain."

There was a pause; then Manny Jacoby spoke quietly. "Do what you have to do." Another pause, but briefer. "Maybe you should have someone with you to confirm your findings."

"I don't like—"

"There are times, Norah, when asking for help is not a sign of weakness."

"I don't want to put anybody on the spot."

"Your friends won't look at it like that. They'll consider it a privilege. And you do have friends."

Norah flushed. "Thanks, Captain. I appreciate that more than I can say."

Yet she was reluctant to ask. The sin of pride. She'd always been guilty of it. This was an opportunity to overcome it. She could call Ferdi; he'd be glad to help. She picked up the phone and dialed. After six rings she hung up, relieved there was no answer. She waited half an hour and tried again. Still no answer. She decided not to tempt fate a third time and called Jocelyn Warran instead. Ms Warran picked up promptly.

Norah introduced herself and then went on. "I'm sorry to disturb you, but I would very much like to talk to you."

"You're not disturbing me, Lieutenant. I'm glad you called."

"I'd like to come over now if it's convenient."

"My time is your time, Lieutenant."

Ms. Warran's cooperation was unexpected and heartening and made the presence of another officer unnecessary. Too bad all witnesses couldn't be like this, Norah thought as she walked the short distance from her apartment to Jocelyn Warran's. Her building was much like Norah's, but larger and with a doorman in front. When she arrived, Norah found the doorman had already been instructed to send her right up. Jocelyn Warran had set out coffee and pastries on the sideboard of a well-appointed dining alcove.

"You shouldn't have gone to this trouble, Ms. Warran."

She was in her mid-twenties, slim, with long, straight brown hair that fell around her shoulders like a shawl. Large hazel eyes dominated her oval face.

"No trouble, no trouble. Please, sit down. Have something. I just feel so bad about the way this thing has turned out. I mean, you saved me. If you hadn't been there . . . if you hadn't called out . . . God knows what would have happened." She shuddered. "I shouldn't have run away. I should have stayed to help you, but I was so shaken."

"That's understandable. And you did come forward."

"To tell you the truth, I only came forward to support you. I feel I owe you. Now it turns out I've made more trouble for you. I'm really sorry. Please, sit down, have a cup of coffee." She picked up the pot and poured.

Norah had to smile. "Maybe you wouldn't mind telling me exactly what happened? I know you've gone over and over it again and again, but . . ."

"I don't mind. Honestly. I have a date with a friend, Abby Thomas, to jog every night after work. She works at the Metropolitan Museum and I work for an art dealer on Madison. We change into our running outfits at the office and meet at the Sixty-seventh Street entrance. Last Friday, Abby called to say she had to work late. It was a bad night and ordinarily that would have been it, but I was feeling kind of down. I really needed the exercise, so I thought, why not? There would be plenty of people around. And if it rained—well, what's a little rain? Why not go anyway?"

She sighed. "I followed our usual route to the Boathouse, but when I got there, the place was deserted, and very dark. I was a little nervous, but at that point there wasn't anything I could do but keep going. So I did. Suddenly, this man came out from behind the men's lavatory and stood in front of me, blocking my way. He was young, clean-cut, good-looking. If I'd met him at a cocktail party, I would have flirted with him.

"He smiled at me. He said, 'Hi, honey. What are you doing out here all by your lonesome?'

" 'I'm not by my lonesome,' I told him. 'I'm meeting my boyfriend.'

" 'Where?' he asked me.

" 'Up ahead.' He kept smiling, and the more he smiled the more nervous I got.

" 'I'll walk with you,' he said.

" 'Thank you, but that's not necessary,' I told him. I stepped to one side and he blocked me. I tried to get by on the other side and he matched that. 'Let me pass,' I said.

" 'If that's what you want. I was only trying to be nice. It's your loss, sweetheart.'

"So he stood over to one side and I breathed a sigh of relief—I thought he was going to let me by. But as I started, he grabbed me by the arm and spun me around. Then he threw his other arm around my throat and pulled me close. I was more startled than anything else till he locked both arms around me and I began to have trouble breathing. I tried to get free, to pull his arms off me, but he was too strong. He was dragging me into the bushes and I was close to blacking out when, by sheer instinct, I reached back and dug my nails into his face. I dug as hard as I could." She held her hands out for Norah to see. "I've always taken pride in my nails."

They were gleaming red, exquisitely manicured, long and sharp—except for the forefinger of her right hand.

"I broke that on him," she said. "He howled and let me go. I took off. I didn't try to get past him this time. I went in the other direction, straight up the hill and into the Ramble."

Jocelyn Warran paused, pulled out a chair and sat opposite Norah. "He came after me. I'd hurt him and I guess he meant to pay me back."

Norah nodded.

"I stopped for a couple of seconds to catch my breath and to figure what to do. I needed to get to where there were people. The best bet was Belvedere Castle, but I had no idea what direction to take. I couldn't see the sky above or the area below. I was lost in a tangle of vegetation. I tell you, Lieutenant, that was the worst moment of all. I could hear him behind me, thrashing through the bushes. I had to do something—anything was better than standing still. I had no idea where I was going, I just plunged ahead. Then I got lucky. I found myself on a high ledge, and below me was the whole panorama of the lake and the skyline of Central Park West.

"I started down the hill, sidestepping carefully, and I almost made it, but at the last moment, when I was nearly at the bottom, my toe caught on something and I pitched forward. That's when he got me by the ankles." She took a deep breath. "Well, you know the rest."

"I'd like to hear it from you."

"I twisted my knee when I fell and I was slow getting up. Then you called out. You announced you were a police officer and you ordered him to let me go. That distracted him just long enough for me to get away."

So far her story supported what Norah had seen and what she had inferred.

"Did he at any time pull a gun on you?"

"No." Jocelyn Warran's large, limpid eyes showed her sympathy. "I'm sorry. If he had a gun, I didn't see it. He didn't use it to intimidate me or anything like that."

That quenched the last flicker of Norah's hope.

"If he'd had a gun, he wouldn't have needed to chase me," the young woman pointed out reluctantly.

"Shooting you was not what he was after."

Jocelyn Warran shivered.

"According to the newspaper accounts, you did hear shots," Norah said.

"Yes, I did."

"How many shots?"

"Two." She answered promptly, eagerly.

She had indeed been over the ground many times, Norah thought. She had been taken over it till she was set in it. "Was there an interval between the shots?"

"Yes." Again the answer was automatic. "The first shot came right after I'd gotten on my feet and started running again. I headed away from both of you toward the main road and the West Side. I didn't want to get caught in the cross fire."

That brought Norah up short. "If he didn't have a gun, how could there be a cross fire?" she asked.

"Oh?" Jocelyn Warran was dismayed. "I saw your gun and I suppose I took it for granted . . . That's not good enough, is it?"

Norah shook her head, hiding her excitement. "How long before you heard the other shot?"

"I had gotten around the bend in the path."

"So you were out of sight. You didn't see what happened?"

"No. I'm sorry. I wish I hadn't run away."

"It was a natural reaction, Ms. Warran," Norah assured her.

Monday, September 28
11:25 p.m.

When she got back to her apartment, the red light was blinking insistently on her answering machine. Norah stared at it. All the anxieties she'd been able to clear away while dealing with the Rocker case, and had held at bay talking to Jocelyn Warran, now returned with a rush. Was this another of those hate calls? She couldn't go on refusing to answer. Sooner or later she'd have to deal with the situation. Heart pounding, she pressed the message button.

There was a whir and a long buzz. Norah waited till the harsh sound stopped and the red light resumed blinking. The caller had hung up without leaving a message. She hated it when they did that. It could have been anybody, she told herself: family, friend, the television repairman she'd been expecting for over a week. Whoever or whatever would have to wait. She sank into her favorite chair, slid down on the end of her spine, kicked off her shoes, and closed her eyes. She would rest for a few minutes . . .

She came to with a start.

The phone was ringing loudly with that hollow, amplified sound caused by the answering machine. For several seconds Norah didn't move. She would let the machine handle it. Then, suddenly, she jumped to her feet. No! Enough was enough. No more hiding. She reached and picked up the receiver before the fourth ring.

"Who is this? What do you want?"

"It's Ferdi, Lieutenant."

"Oh. I'm sorry. I was asleep and I thought . . . I'm sorry. What's up?"

"Homicide, Lieutenant. Another one of The Earth Shakers. Duggie Watts."

"The sound engineer."

"Right. He was killed in his room at the Park West. Shot twice. In the back both times."

"How did you know I was back?" Norah asked.

"Captain Jacoby said to call you."

"I'm on my way."

Tuesday, September 29
2:05 a.m.

The small, twin-bedded room overlooked a courtyard. It was dark and gloomy. As he and Norah entered, Ferdi turned the ceiling light on. By its harsh glare, the second-rate appointments looked third rate.

The victim lay sprawled on the floor in front of a combination writing desk and vanity. As Ferdi had told her, he'd been shot in the back, and he was now lying on his stomach, head turned sideways as though he were looking over his shoulder to see who had done it. Bending down for a closer look, Norah noted the two entry wounds—neat, side by side, with little external bleeding. Ferdi had called her before making the routine notifications, so no one from the M.E.'s office or Forensics had arrived. The usual number of uniforms were in the doorway and milling in the corridor.

"Who found him?" Norah asked.

"His roommate, Rollo Dubois. Came back from a movie, walked into the room, saw him, and screamed the place down."

"Where's Dubois now?"

"Waiting in an empty room down the hall. Whenever you want to talk to him . . ."

"In a minute." Norah took another long look at the victim. Aside from the fact that his upper body was well developed but his legs were short, there was nothing unusual about him. He was wearing dark trousers and an expensive hand-knit cardigan over a plain white shirt. Low-key. He didn't belong with singers and musicians. Yet Bo Russell had sought him out for the job, encouraged him to acquire the necessary skills. It was another example of Bo's loyalty to his friends.

She took a slow tour of the room. She looked in the closets, opened bureau drawers, found and examined a small pocket diary and a worn brown leather wallet. It contained ID with Watts's home address, driver's license, a ten-dollar bill and five singles. It also contained every credit card Norah had ever heard of.

"Okay. Let's talk to the roommate." She gestured for Ferdi to lead the way.

The room was similar to the one they'd just left except that it was made up and therefore showed to better advantage. Rollo Dubois stood at the window, looking out into the courtyard at other windows with their shades drawn. At Norah and Ferdi's entrance, he turned. He had stopped crying, but his eyes were red and swollen, and the tears had left streaks down his cheeks.

"I'm very sorry about your friend," Norah said.

He nodded. "Thank you."

"I'm sorry to intrude on your grief, but there are questions I need to ask."

"I understand."

"Thank you." Norah pulled out a chair and sat down opposite, giving him time to collect himself. Ferdi perched at the end of one of the twin beds.

"Have you any idea who could have done this?" she asked.

"No."

"Or why?"

"No. Duggie never hurt anybody. He was gentle. And generous. Give you the shirt off his back. Everybody liked him."

At least one person didn't, Norah thought. "Are you suggesting certain persons owed him money?"

"No, no." He was flustered. "It was a manner of speaking, that's all."

"He was shot in his own room and well away from the door. He was also shot in the back. The two together suggest he was at ease with his killer."

This elicited no comment from Dubois.

"When was the last time you saw your roommate alive, Mr. Dubois?" Norah wanted to know.

Dubois seemed neither surprised nor threatened by the question. "We had dinner together. There's a little place around the corner we like . . . we used to like."

"And then what did you do?"

"I went to the movies."

"Alone?"

"Yes."

"What did Mr. Watts do?"

"He went back to the room."

Norah paused for a moment. "According to nine-one-one, your call reporting the homicide was received at five minutes after one this morning. Movies don't usually run that late."

"That's right. The movie let out before midnight. I stopped for a nightcap downstairs."

"Will anyone remember you?"

"The bartender should. He served me with a dirty glass. I called him on it."

"Fortuitous," she remarked.

Dubois flushed. "He would have remembered me anyway—I've been in there a dozen times within the last few days. We all have."

Norah didn't argue. "How long have you and Mr. Watts been rooming together?"

"Since the start of the tour."

"How did you happen to get together?"

"We both needed to cut down on expenses."

"You make good money, don't you?"

"But it goes . . . somehow."

Not for accommodations like this, Norah thought. "You did say Mr. Watts was generous. Did he also gamble?"

Dubois bit his lip. "Sometimes."

"How about drugs?"

"No, no drugs. Never. Bo won't tolerate drugs."

Norah let that go, for now. "Why didn't Mr. Watts go to the movie with you?"

"He had something else on." Dubois hesitated, then took the plunge. "I wasn't particularly interested in the movie myself. I went to oblige him."

Now it was getting interesting, Norah thought. "So he was expecting a visitor. A woman?"

"It wasn't for sex. Duggie wouldn't have brought a woman to the room for sex. It was business."

"What kind of business?"

"Somebody owed him money from way back and was finally going to pay up. He said we'd be able to clear out all our bills and get solvent again."

"Both of you?"

The singer shrugged. "I lent Duggie some money a while back. I wasn't in any hurry for it. I told him not to worry about it. Of course, he had other creditors."

"Bookies?"

Dubois nodded.

So Duggie Watts needed money. "This person who owed your friend from way back, as you say . . . It doesn't seem to me that it was necessary to send you away for most of the night to collect payment for an old debt. On the other hand, if Mr. Watts was engaged in black-mail—"

"No!"

"The thought has occurred to you, I see."

"No."

The denial was less vehement the second time, Norah thought. "If you have any idea what he knew that could have been a threat to anyone, you should tell us right here and now. If you're thinking of putting the squeeze on this person yourself, don't. You could end up like your roommate." She handed the singer her card. "When you're ready, call me. Anytime."

Chapter 14

Tuesday, September 29
7:35 a.m.

The morning editions devoted varying amounts of space to the murder of the sound engineer. Had he been a performer, there would have been more coverage. Norah was mentioned as heading the Rocker investigation, of which this killing was certainly a part. There was only an offhand reference to the fact that she was under a cloud regarding the shooting of the alleged mugger in Central Park. In some accounts, that wasn't even mentioned. She knew this was only a temporary respite.

From the Park West Hotel, she had gone directly to the squad. It was time to take up the reins again. She'd only been absent for a couple of days but it seemed longer. Resuming active command would show confidence. If she didn't believe in herself and in her own innocence, how could she expect others to do so? As she passed through the room, she was greeted with various degrees of warmth and awkwardness. She stopped at Al Sutphin's desk.

"I see by the papers that George Koster's intended victim has come forward and identified herself," she said.

"Jocelyn Warran. That's right."

175

"She says that as far as she could tell, he didn't have a gun. At least he didn't threaten her with a gun."

"Yeah. That's what she says. I'm sorry, Lieutenant."

"No you're not."

He flinched. The detectives who overheard gasped.

"What do you intend to do next?" she continued.

"About the case? What else is there?"

"You could go deeper into Koster's background. You could find out if he had a steady girlfriend now or in the past. Talk to her about the nature of the relationship. Talk to his parents. The neighbors. All elementary, Detective."

Sutphin's eyes smoldered.

"We know Koster was licensed to carry," Norah went on. "If he didn't have the piece on him that night, then where was it? What did he do with it? He must have left it somewhere. At home? In the office? Why haven't you looked?"

"If he didn't have it on him, what difference does it make where it was? It isn't going to help you. In fact, the opposite," Sutphin countered boldly.

Everybody stopped whatever he was doing. There was not even a pretense of working.

"Maybe not," Norah enunciated clearly. "But before I'm convicted of shooting down an unarmed man, I want to know everything I can about him."

"I don't blame you for that."

"Thank you. You may care to know that I.A. did toss both Koster's home and office and found no weapon."

Sutphin shrugged.

"Jocelyn Warran mentioned she was fearful of getting caught in a cross fire. Did she say anything about that to you?"

"You've talked to her?" Sutphin stiffened, jaw clenched till his temples visibly throbbed. "I thought this was my case. I should have been with you."

176

"I'm in command of the squad," she reminded him. "If you're unhappy about my methods, go to the captain. Go higher if you want. Go all the way." It was not Norah's custom to dress a man down in the presence of his peers, nor to challenge him. And she wasn't through.

"About the García case—the D.A. expects the grand jury will reduce the charge against Luisa to manslaughter. A deal could bring it down to man two. The sentence could be limited to extended probation." She waited for his comment. When it became evident he wasn't going to make any, she motioned Arenas and the others on the Rocker case into her office.

It left Al Sutphin alone in the squad room. It was the final humiliation.

With the men she trusted around her, Norah reviewed the latest developments in the case—specifically, the murder of Duggie Watts. She outlined what had to be done and made the assignments.

The Earth Shakers consisted of sixteen performers— backup singers and musicians. Spouses and girlfriends traveled with them. They had all been interrogated once; they had to be interrogated again. House engineers and technicians present in Studio A on the morning of Ben Russell's murder were not likely suspects, but couldn't be ignored. With Wyler in the hospital and Ochs working on the books, the team was now reduced to Arenas, Neel, and Tedesco. She considered taking more men off the chart and decided against it. She intended to handle the second round of interrogation of the principals herself, starting as before with Ellie Lyras.

"The medical examiner has fixed the time of Duggie Watts's death at somewhere between eleven p.m. and one a.m.," Norah told the agent.

"And you want to know where I was? I was home, in

bed—alone," she added with a smile that was both gentle and sad.

She was a lovely lady, Norah thought, kind and caring. Her unusual height and the ultraconservative way she dressed were off-putting. It kept people from seeing her inner beauty.

"Most innocent people don't have ready alibis," Norah assured her. "What can you tell me about Duggie Watts?"

"He wasn't a performer, so I had little to do with him. I only know what everybody else knows. He was orphaned like Bo and Ben. The three of them were in the same foster home for a while. Inevitably, they were split up, but they didn't lose touch. When he hit it big and organized his own group, Bo wanted to help Duggie. Duggie had no artistic talent, so Bo encouraged him to study sound engineering and paid for the course. Then he hired Duggie to be his personal mix engineer. The life got to Duggie, of course, as it does to most—the money, the glamour. . . . Bo is one of the few I know who have remained unaffected."

"According to his roomie, Duggie Watts gambled," Norah said.

"He did," the agent agreed. "I know because he tried to hit me for a couple thou to pay off his debts. I didn't have it. If I had, I wouldn't have given it to him."

"Do you think he would have resorted to blackmail?"

"I don't know. It would depend on how heavy the pressure was on him to pay up." Eleanor Lyras sighed. "In my opinion, he would have had to go outside the group. Everybody in the group is broke."

Except for the manager, Norah thought. The manager was in a position where he could always get hold of some cash.

*   *   *

Tieless, in shirtsleeves, surrounded by stacks of papers, Herb Cranston appeared not to have made much progress since the last time she'd seen him.

"I need to talk to you about Duggie Watts."

The two chairs he'd called for on that other occasion were folded in a corner. Cranston got one and set it out for her.

"I'm at your disposal, Lieutenant."

"According to the medical examiner, Duggie Watts died sometime between eleven last night and one this morning. Where were you at that time, Mr. Cranston?"

"Right here, in bed and asleep," he answered readily. "We work late hours, so an early night is appreciated."

"Of course. Did you make or receive any telephone calls?"

"I was asleep, Lieutenant," he reminded.

"That means you didn't. The floor maid says she saw you coming in around one."

"She's mistaken."

He remained unperturbed. His boldly carved features and the suggestion of physical strength they imparted added conviction to his statement.

"I appreciate your cooperation in giving Detective Ochs access to the company books."

"Glad to help."

"Thank you. Both Detective Ochs and I have questions."

"Regarding what?"

"Unreported income."

"There is none." He smiled broadly, obviously relieved. "Bo Russell receives income from many sources. In addition to record sales and box office receipts from concerts, there are endorsements, product commercials. Bo has investments in a southern food chain and a network of service stations. I make full disclosure, Lieutenant. I don't want to tangle with the I.R.S., believe me."

She did believe him. It had been in the nature of a probe and also a diversion.

"We're talking about separate income here, right? Apart from what comes in by way of The Earth Shakers?"

"And what goes out. Don't forget what goes out, Lieutenant. I wanted Bo to incorporate the group. That would have limited his liability and sheltered his outside earnings. He wouldn't hear of it. The Earth Shakers is a part of him and he is one with the group. He wanted to retain full and unilateral control."

"The story we get, Mr. Cranston, is that The Earth Shakers leave a string of creditors in every town." Norah was jabbing him here and there, hoping to fluster him. "If money is coming in from private investments, why aren't the bills getting paid? Where's the money going? The logical answer is—into somebody's pocket."

"The *obvious* answer, Lieutenant, is that the money coming in is insufficient," he corrected.

"Then you won't mind if we take a look at Bo's personal bank statements?"

"I'll make them available, but you won't find anything. I'm not a thief and I'm not stupid."

"I'll tell you how it looks to us, Mr. Cranston. It's part of your job to check the box office receipts every night Bo and the group appear in concert. Ben was working with you, ostensibly to learn but very possibly to check on you. And he caught you. He caught you skimming and threatened to tell his brother unless you cut him in. So you killed him."

There was not so much as a crack in Cranston's granite facade.

"Then Duggie Watts found out. He approached you

and also threatened to go to Bo. So you had to kill him, too."

"Are you making this up as you go along, Lieutenant? It sounds like it."

Norah shook her head. "I've done a lot of thinking these past days and I've come to the conclusion that you are very loyal to Bo Russell and that you would do anything for him, including lying for him."

He didn't comment.

"It was three forty-five in the morning when Bo contacted you and ordered the recording session to resume at five. Assuming you called Ben first and you did reach him as you claim, that left over an hour for him to dress and get to the studio where he met his killer. An argument ensued which climaxed in murder. Some additional time was necessary for the perpetrator to place the body inside the isolation booth. It could have happened that way, but, somehow, it doesn't feel right.

"On the other hand, suppose when you called his room, there was no answer. Suppose Ben wasn't there. It would have been logical for you to try other places, other hangouts. In between calling the others, you kept trying to locate Ben. Finally you tried the studio. You knew he had a key—he might well be there. And he was. You were relieved. You gave him the message and went on with the rest of the calls. That done, you went to the studio yourself and were surprised not to see him. Of course, when Bo got there he wanted to know if you'd contacted Ben, and you said you had. You didn't go into detail. Bo knew his brother used the studio for his own purposes—so did everybody else—but once you'd committed yourself, you had to stick to your story."

"Okay. I admit it. I did lie. Is it important?"

"Everything is important in a murder investigation."

"I didn't want to embarrass Bo."

"It seems everybody wants to protect Bo," Norah remarked. "He's their meal ticket, but they also like and respect him. Am I right?"

"Yes."

"So you lied about having reached Ben in his room merely to spare Bo embarrassment?"

"I didn't think it would make any difference."

"And when you finally did reach Ben Russell, he was already at the studio?"

"Yes."

"And where were you?"

"Here. Right here, in my room."

"Not the studio?"

"No. Absolutely not. I made all the calls from right here and I stayed on the phone till I had contacted every single performer and technician. It took more than half an hour. I asked for an outside line to contact those who weren't living in the hotel. You can check the hotel operator."

"I will," Norah said.

Strike Herb Cranston, she thought.

Tuesday, September 29
2:00 p.m.

The first time she and Ferdi interviewed Helene Galinas they'd gone easy on her, Norah thought. They had strolled into the Park West coffee shop where she worked and casually engaged her in conversation. The idea had been to put her at her ease. Ferdi was particularly good at gaining a witness's confidence, but Galinas, young as she was, hadn't succumbed.

This time it would be different.

She considered taking the waitress to the precinct to give her a taste of reality. But the bleak interrogation room and the presence of the official stenographer might cause the girl to freeze up. So Norah compromised by arranging to use the assistant manager's office and having Helene Galinas brought in.

"Sit down." She gestured to a chair in front of the desk at which she was seated.

The waitress did as she was told, glancing curiously at Ferdi, who sat at one side with pad and pencil.

"You remember Sergeant Arenas," Norah said. "He'll be taking notes." No tape recorder—too daunting.

Ferdi looked up, and there was none of the easy friendliness he'd shown at the first interview.

Nor was Helene the fresh, carefree girl she had been. Her complexion was sallow. The circles under her eyes were like smudges, broad and dark, seemingly permanent. The bounce was gone.

"We want to make sure there's no mistake about your statement. It's for your own protection," Norah explained.

Helene Galinas nodded, but she didn't appear reassured.

"You were not exactly honest with us the last time, Miss Galinas," Norah chided.

She didn't deny it. She didn't attempt to justify herself either. She sat there waiting to see just what she was in for before looking for a way to get out of it. A shrewd and conniving little girl.

"You told us that on the night he was killed, Ben Russell called you and urged you to meet him for a late date. You said that you agreed but that when you got here and went up to his room and knocked, there was no answer."

"That's right."

"You said he left a note for you at the desk. In the note he told you to meet him at Triumph Studios, that the back door would be open for you. But when you got there, it was locked."

"It was locked and I went away."

"No, it wasn't locked and you didn't go away. We have a witness who saw you in Studio A with Ben Russell right about four a.m."

"Who?" she challenged.

"We're not accusing you of having anything to do with the murder," Norah assured her.

"Who?" the waitress insisted.

"You were there. You tell us," Norah retorted. "Do you realize that person could be the killer? If you know who it is, do you realize the danger you're in?"

This time Helene Galinas was silent.

"You're afraid and I don't blame you," Norah said. "But if you think keeping silent will protect you, you're wrong. Your only protection is to tell us what you know."

Helene paled, but she pressed her lips tightly together as though to prevent any word from slipping through.

Norah sighed. "All right, let me tell you how it looks. You went to the studio as Ben instructed you to do. You tried the back door and it was open. You went upstairs where Ben was waiting. You made love and, in the midst of it, the phone rang. It was Herb Cranston, the manager. He warned Ben that Bo had called a recording session and the group would be arriving at any time. The two of you got dressed as fast as you could and Ben hustled you down the stairs and out the back."

The girl remained silent, neither accepting nor denying.

"Your boyfriend, Vinnie, was jealous and suspected what was going on. He had followed you from your home to the hotel and to the studio. When he saw the two of you come out and Ben put you in a taxi, he drew the obvious conclusion. As soon as the taxi drove off, he grabbed Ben."

"No! Vinnie wasn't there. He wasn't anywhere near there. Honestly."

"Ben was a big man, but Vinnie was bigger, younger, stronger. He grabbed Ben and hit him." Norah continued the reconstruction. "Somehow, Ben managed to stay on his feet and run back into the building. He tried to shut the door on Vinnie, but he wasn't fast enough. Vinnie got inside and chased him up the stairs and into Studio A. He gave Ben Russell the beating of his life."

It wasn't true; there had been no bruises on Ben's body. The rest of it was fabrication too, but Helene didn't know that.

"I don't know who told you I was at the studio, but I know it wasn't Vinnie. He would never tell on me."

"Who do you think did?" Norah asked.

Helene Galinas hesitated, then took the plunge. "Her. Mrs. Russell." She spit out the name as though it were a foul taste in her mouth.

"You saw Gloria Russell in the studio that night?" Norah covered her excitement.

"I didn't exactly see her. I heard her. I heard her calling for Ben as we were leaving."

"She called from inside?"

"Yes."

She must have had a key too, Norah thought. Some lockout! "If you didn't see her, what makes you think it was Mrs. Russell?"

"I recognized her voice."

Norah had hoped for better. "What makes you think she knew you were there?"

"She knew for sure Ben wasn't alone. She'd walked in

on us in his room at the hotel when we were fooling around, so she could make a pretty good guess. She was jealous as sin."

"She walked in on you?"

"That's right."

She was not ashamed. Far from it; she was proud. "Why didn't you tell us this before?"

"I didn't want Vinnie to know."

"But he did know!" Norah exploded in frustration. "He'd caught you coming out of Ben Russell's room and demanded an explanation. You admitted everything and promised to stay away from Ben. You swore. You told us that."

"I didn't want him to know I broke my promise." She bowed her head. "Thing is, Ben had promised to help me make a demo tape. That's why I came in that night. That's why I got involved with him in the first place. It was a chance to make something of myself."

"You're a singer?"

"I'm as good as a lot of them up there. Millions, they're making. Millions. For what? They can't sing, they can't act. Some are downright ugly. This was a chance for me, maybe the only one I'd ever get. Ben promised, but he kept putting me off. I made up my mind he was going to come through. If he didn't, I was going straight to Bo. Ben didn't want that, so he called to say we could get the use of the studio. I wasn't thrilled with going back to Manhattan at that hour, but what could I do? Pretty soon Ben and the whole group would be moving on."

She paused briefly. "When the phone in the control room rang, we weren't making love. We were recording."

The lure of fame, Norah thought.

Helene Galinas went back to work. Norah Mulcahaney and Ferdi Arenas sat a while longer in the assistant manager's office.

"It could have been Vinnie," Ferdi reasoned. "He didn't know or care whether or not they were *recording*. They were together, Ben and Helene, that was all that mattered. Having seen Helene come out of the singer's room once was enough. He got himself a gun and when he followed her back to Manhattan on Tuesday night, he took it with him."

"So why didn't he use it right away?" Norah asked. "Why did he wait till Ben got back inside the building and then follow him upstairs? Why didn't he kill him right then and there on the street?"

"Because Helene and the taxi driver were witnesses."

"All right. So after they were gone, Vinnie followed Ben up to the studio and shot him there. Why take the trouble to hide the body? Why drag it into the isolation booth? To give Helene time to get away? She was already gone." Norah answered her own question.

"To give himself time. No, he had no connection to Ben Russell. He was not likely to be suspected." Ferdi posed the question and answered it as Norah had done.

They looked at each other.

Strike Helene Galinas.

Strike Vinnie DeCicco.

"Why should Gloria Russell have cared about Helene's relationship with Ben?" Norah wondered. "The way Helene tells it, she was insanely jealous. We know Gloria was Ben's girlfriend before she married Bo. There's no secret about it."

"That's something like five years ago," Ferdi pointed out. "He's had plenty of other women in between. It didn't seem to bother her. Why should it suddenly bother her now?"

Wednesday, September 30
Noon

Bo Russell had to rehearse all day Tuesday and declined to be interviewed by the police. Husband and wife slept late Wednesday.

The remains of brunch were on the room-service cart in the sitting room of their suite. They faced each other over black coffee. Bo wore his standard jeans and turtle-neck pullover. Gloria still hadn't dressed. She wore a skimpy red satin teddy under a black see-through neg-ligee.

"One cigarette, Bo. Come on, can't I have just one?"

"You know you won't stop at one."

"Yes I will. I promise."

He was patient. "The doctor says you should get out and get some fresh air and exercise. What do you say we take a little walk together?"

"I don't want to." She pouted. I don't feel so good." The shadows under her eyes were shaded black to blue. Her hair was frowsy, the blond color washed out, the roots showing black.

"You've got to take better care of yourself, sweetheart."

"That's easy for you to say—you don't throw up every morning."

"You'll feel better once you get outside. We'll stroll over to Fifth and take a look at Bergdorf's. What do you say?"

For the first time there was a spark of interest in his wife's eyes. "They're having a sale."

"Good. We'll check it out," he promised.

At that point the phone rang.

"Oh, Lieutenant Mulcahaney . . . Well, we're just about to go out, but since you're in the lobby . . . All

right, come on up." He replaced the receiver. "That
was—"

"I don't want to talk to her," Gloria said.

"It's probably about Duggie."

"I don't care. I don't want to talk to her about Duggie
or anybody. I'm not up to it, Bo. I'm just not up to it."
Her face puckered like a cranky child's. She was on the
verge of tears. "Please, Bo, do I have to?"

"All right, all right. You go on in and lie down. I'll
take care of it." There was a light knock. "That's her."
Gently, he propelled his wife toward her bedroom and
waited till she'd closed the door behind her before ad-
mitting Norah.

Norah was alone this time, hoping the Russells would
feel less threatened. She noted the partially consumed
meal on the cart, the general disarray of the room, and
took particular interest in the fact that the oversized
teddy bear Russell had brought home a few days ago
still occupied the place of honor on the sofa.

"Sorry to disturb you, Mr. Russell." She looked point-
edly at the closed bedroom door.

He felt constrained to explain. "Gloria isn't feeling so
good. Morning sickness."

Well past morning, Norah thought. "I'm sorry. I
understood you to say the two of you were on your way
out."

"I'm on my way out. Just me," he corrected. "I'm sure
I can answer whatever questions you have for us."

"I'm sure you can. If you will."

"What does that mean?"

"Your people have been less than honest, Mr. Russell,"
she told him almost regretfully. "Actually, they've been
lying—not for themselves, it seems, but for you. They
seem to feel you need protecting. Why is that?"

"I have no idea. I don't think it's true."

189

"Your manager, Herb Cranston, lied about how he contacted your brother on the night he was killed. He said he reached Ben in his hotel room on the first try. He now admits Ben didn't answer and it took a while before he finally tracked him down at the studio."

"What difference does that make?"

"Considerable. For one thing, it places Ben at the scene of his death a lot earlier. Ben was known to use the various studios you rented for assignations with women. Apparently he had one such that Wednesday morning when he was killed."

Bo scowled.

"It was no secret to your manager or your agent, or the rest of the group for that matter. I see it was no secret to you either."

"He was my brother. He took care of me when we were kids. He fought to keep us together."

"And you've never stopped paying him back. It's commendable, but it can be carried too far."

"That's your opinion."

"What I don't understand is your present attitude. You don't seem to care how or why he died. Don't you want to find his killer?"

"Of course I do."

"All right then. Let's talk about Duggie Watts for a moment, and be straight with me, please. On the night Duggie died, where were you between eleven p.m. and one a.m.?"

"Me? Here. I was right here watching television."

"Alone?"

"With my wife, naturally."

"Nobody else?"

"No."

She paused and then asked what was becoming the standard question. "Why do you think Watts was killed?"

"I suppose because he knew something that was a threat to whoever killed Ben."

"Yes, that's the line we're pursuing. Duggie Watts confirmed that you arrived at the studio with a key to let the artists in shortly after four-thirty. Ben had already been shot, of course, and his body placed in the isolation booth. But suppose Watts, like Cranston, was lying to protect you, only this time at a price?"

"Since I have keys both to the back and the front doors of the studio building, the lie would be useless."

"True," Norah agreed. "A lot of people had keys."

"So it's hardly a basis for blackmail," Bo pointed out. "I didn't kill my brother. How many times do I have to say it?"

"Gloria was your brother's girlfriend before you married her."

"So?" He was wary.

"Your people are loyal and were careful to steer clear of the subject. But once I found out . . ."

"How did you find out?"

"Actually, your wife told me."

"Gloria?" He was stunned.

"The very first time I talked with her, in fact. She told me she'd been going steady with your brother for a couple of years, but the relationship had no future. She told me that you went to him and asked him his intentions. When he said he didn't have any, you asked if he'd mind if you dated her. She told me about your beautiful wedding and all the famous people who attended."

His face softened. "So?"

"She also mentioned that Ben was at the wedding, that he drank too much and made passes at all the young girls."

"For Ben that was pretty much standard."

"Why should she have made a point of telling me about it?"

"For that very reason. Because it was standard for Ben."

Norah shook her head. "She had been going with him for two years. Old feelings die hard. You're all thrown together: you travel together, perform together, live in the same hotel. You've built homes within a stone's throw of each other. Time seems to have hung heavy on your wife's hands. Maybe at last the old fires were rekindled."

Bo Russell drew himself up. His round, youthful face took on a grave dignity. He spoke with quiet assurance. "They wouldn't do that. I know they were intimate be-fore—I accepted that. But not since. No. Not Ben and not Gloria. They wouldn't betray me. I know Gloria doesn't have enough to occupy her. I know she's been bored and restless. But now she's going to have a baby and all that will change. So. That's all I have to say to you, Lieutenant." He walked her to the door and held it for her.

Chapter 15

At the end of the shift, the team gathered in Norah's office. They sat in their accustomed places, in their characteristic poses. Norah was at her desk, the reports of alibis covering the period of Duggie Watts's death piled at her left. She gestured toward them.

"Anything startling or unexpected?" she asked.

There was a general murmur of dissent.

"I may have something," she told them, "but first I want to review a couple of points. From the start the problem with this case has been that we didn't really know what happened. A man, the brother of a big rock star, was shot and killed. We found him in a booth—called an isolation booth by musicians. It's slightly larger than an old-fashioned telephone booth. There were no powder marks on the victim, so that suggests he wasn't killed in the booth but was put there afterward. Presumably, it was done because there was no time to get rid of the body. Okay so far?"

She looked around and all, including Ochs, nodded.

"Next, we needed to know what the victim, Ben Russell, was doing in that studio at that hour of the morning.

Bo Russell, the star, paid a lot of money to have exclusive access to the studio so he could go in and work by himself or call a full rehearsal and recording session with his backup singers, the band, and a fully manned control room whenever he felt like it. If he was composing and didn't require any of the electronic equipment, Bo liked to work in his room. Everybody knew his work habits. Certainly, Ben did. When he knew his brother was composing, he used the studio to entertain his women. He enticed them with the promise of making a demo tape to display their talent and help them to break into the music business.

"In the early hours of September twenty-third, Bo Russell was working in his room at the Park West Hotel on a new song that was giving him a lot of trouble. The creative flow had stopped. He was blocked and desperate. Suddenly the logjam broke. The backup of inspiration rushed through in a flood. He put as much of it on paper as he could, but then he needed not only the electronic equipment but his singers and the band. He called his manager to get everybody together for a session. He was excited, eager to work. He had no idea what time it was—he didn't care.

"The manager stated originally that the first person he called, as a matter of protocol, was Ben Russell, and that Ben was in his room and he answered. Cranston lied."

No one said a word, but there was no doubt of the heightened interest.

"Cranston has now changed his story. He now says he did call Ben's room first, but there was no answer. Then he tried several of Ben's known hangouts without success. Finally he tried the studio. Ben was there. I think we can take it he was with a woman. In fact, the waitress, Helene Galinas, admits to being that woman.

"Upon getting the call, he didn't waste any time putting her out the back door."

"And somebody saw him." Tedesco jumped in. "The boyfriend. What's his name? Vinnie."

"Suppose it wasn't Vinnie?"

Tedesco frowned.

Neel grinned. "The waitress saw who it was."

"She says it was Gloria Russell," Norah told them.

It produced only a mild surprise. These men were accustomed to the unexpected, to twisted motives.

"What was she doing there?" Ochs asked.

"According to the waitress, she was jealous. She went there to catch the two of them *in flagrante*."

Ochs merely raised his eyebrows.

"She still had the hots for the brother-in-law, eh? Why not?" Tedesco said. "Can the waitress prove it was Gloria Russell she saw?"

"Unfortunately, she didn't actually see Mrs. Russell. She only heard her voice," Norah replied.

"Ah well . . ." Tedesco dismissed it with one of his expressive shrugs.

The others indicated agreement.

"Don't give up so fast," Norah chided. "There may be a way to prove it."

Instantly the atmosphere changed. The team grinned at Norah and at each other. The lieut' had that gleam in her eye and tilt of the chin they knew so well. But they were disappointed. What she proposed was a routine search of Duggie Watts's room for the evidence on which he'd based the blackmail demand.

Then she told them what the evidence was.

She also wanted to toss the Russells' suite. She had already secured the warrants for both, and intended that they be conducted consecutively and openly. She didn't care whether the occupants were present or not; the plan would work either way. After discussion, it was decided it would be as well to have the parties present, and both jobs were scheduled for eleven the next morning. Performers slept late; it was likely the suspects would be not only in their rooms but just getting out of bed.

Neel and Ochs were to go through the room occupied by Watts and Dubois. Tedesco and Arenas would go to the Russells' suite. Both teams were to be courteous and avoid structural damage to hotel property. They were not to open up the upholstery or slash pillows and mattresses. They could, however, take up carpets and sound floorboards, remove pictures from the walls, and examine the backs. They were to appear ruthless, but not do anything that could result in the department's being sued. This was not a SWAT operation.

Thursday, October 1
11:00 a.m.

Through it all Rollo Dubois sat in silence and watched. The moment the detectives were through, he began to collect his roommate's belongings, fold his underwear and pajamas and socks and put them in drawers, restore order. Then, suddenly, he stopped and began to cry.

"I'm sorry," Norah said.

Rollo Dubois turned his head away.

Through it all Bo Russell stood rigid, white-faced with indignation. Without a word, he watched as the detectives went through his personal belongings. When they started handling his wife's things, however, dumping the contents of bureau drawers, piling satin and lace lingerie on the bed, overturning boxes of hats and scarves, he protested.

"What are you looking for?" he demanded. "At least tell me that."

"Relax, Mr. Russell," Norah said. "So far we haven't found it."

She started out of the bedroom and, passing through the sitting room, stopped in front of the giant teddy bear on the sofa. The golden-brown toy sat serenely amidst the chaos. She held her hand out to Ferdi. "Let me have your knife."

"Ah, no . . ." Russell pleaded.

"I'm sorry." Norah inserted the tip of the knife into the toy's back. With one hard pull, she opened it up. Putting her hand inside, she pulled out wads of white stuffing.

"You didn't have to do that," Russell said.

Thursday, October 1
1:30 p.m.

Norah wanted the two searches principally for the effect on the suspects. As for finding the tape, if you believed in "The Purloined Letter," the most likely place for it would be among other tapes recorded by The Earth Shakers during their sessions in New York. It was evidence like any other, and Norah got a warrant authorizing her to listen. It would take hours, she thought, hours that could be shared with the team. She knew they'd be willing, but she didn't want to expose them to the charge of entrapment. She did, however, absolutely need the help of a sound engineer.

She called Jack Haines. Young, eager, energetic, he

worked for Fidelity Network, as Randall Tye had once. Randall had trusted Haines, and Norah had no qualms confiding in him. She couldn't have hoped for a more positive response. He agreed with her reasoning, and agreed that the theory alone wouldn't be enough. They met at Triumph Studio A and together sat through four and a half hours of rock and roll, and country. Haines eased down on the volume to spare Norah the assault of sound. Even so, it was a physical as well as emotional relief to have it finally shut off.

"I don't know how you can take it." She leaned back wearily and removed the headphones.

"We're used to it." He looked hard at her. "So, Lieutenant, you want to go ahead?"

"I do. How about you?"

"I'm game. But we shouldn't do it here. The word could get around. I'll set us up at my place."

"Right. Thanks." Norah took a deep breath and called Ferdi. "We'll meet you at Fidelity. If the girl gives you any trouble, tell her she'll get another chance to make that demo."

"Right."

"That's a promise, Ferdi. If I have to pay for it out of my own pocket. Make sure she understands."

"I will."

"And fast, Ferdi. We haven't got much time." Norah hung up. "They should be there within the half hour," she told Haines. Once again, doubts assailed her. "Are you sure you're okay with this?"

"Hey, I'm just laying tracks. I'm not responsible for how you use them." He winked.

The phone rang. It was Manny Jacoby. "How's it going?"

"No luck, Captain. We're going to have to make the tape."

Jacoby was silent for several moments. "I don't know, Norah. Maybe we shouldn't."

She wasn't surprised at his reluctance. Manny Jacoby was a stickler for procedure. She was surprised he'd gone along this far. Probably he'd agreed in the hope the evidence would turn up. As it hadn't, he was having second thoughts.

"I'm not crazy about it either, but the group is leaving tomorrow. Once they go . . ."

"They're not fleeing the country!" he exclaimed. "They're only going out to Queens, for God's sake. We can go out to Shea and run it through, or at their next stop, wherever that is, or the one after that."

"It won't have the same effect as it will here, now, and in the studio where it happened."

Jacoby's sigh indicated he had given in. "Inspector Mekworth wants you in his office tomorrow at two p.m." Mekworth was I.A. Division in charge of the Central Park shooting case.

She knew better than to ask, but she asked anyway. "Would he grant me a postponement in view of the critical juncture of the Rocker investigation?"

"I already made the request. Mekworth pointed out that you've had two postponements already. They feel any additional special treatment would reflect on their integrity."

Norah gasped. She hadn't known about the earlier summonses. What Manny Jacoby was telling her was that somebody high up had already interceded for her. Jim Felix probably. It was like him to act quietly, without saying anything; he didn't look for gratitude. She couldn't ask him to get the date of the I.A. interrogation set back once more. She had to take care of it herself.

"I need time to prepare my defense," she pointed out.

"They feel you've had plenty of time. How you used it was up to you."

How I wasted it, Norah thought. "So I'm okay till tomorrow afternoon at two, right, Captain?"

"Right. I'll be there. Along with the association lawyer. Incidentally, he's been trying to get hold of you."

She hadn't even thought of notifying the union's attorney. That Jacoby had and was also going to be at the hearing in person touched her. "Thank you, Captain."

Before leaving, Norah signaled the rest of the team to go ahead with their assignments.

Tedesco called on the Russells.

"Lieutenant Mulcahaney has new evidence in the matter of your brother's death, Mr. Russell," he explained. "She'd appreciate it if you would come over to the studio with me. There are a couple of points she needs to clear before wrapping it up."

"Well, I don't know . . . This isn't a convenient time. We're leaving tomorrow morning and, as you see, we've still got packing to do."

Open suitcases and boxes overflowed with gaudy garments that were mostly women's. Bo's costumes would be with the theatrical baggage, Tedesco reasoned. Despite their short stay, Gloria Russell had acquired a lot of possessions, he thought. Of course, Russell didn't have to agree to accompany him to the studio. He could flat-out refuse and there was nothing Tedesco or the lieut' could do about it. The lieut' had made a point of that. She could come over here and conduct the interrogation, but it would be a lot more effective in the studio the way she'd planned it.

"What does Lieutenant Mulcahaney want?" Bo asked. "Can't you give me some idea?"

Tedesco suppressed a smile. The lieut' had advised

him to be vague, counting on Russell's curiosity to tip the balance. "She didn't tell me, but it shouldn't take long. I've got my car downstairs. I'll get you and Mrs. Russell over and back in no time."

"Mrs. Russell? What do you want her for? She doesn't know anything about what happened. She wasn't in the studio. She was here, in bed and asleep."

"The lieutenant suggested Mrs. Russell might want to come along. I can't say why." In fact, he didn't know.

"The lieutenant is mistaken. My wife doesn't want to go anywhere. She's not feeling well."

"I'm sorry." Be polite, the lieut' had instructed. "Lieutenant Mulcahaney certainly wouldn't want to endanger Mrs. Russell's health. She could come here, if that's more convenient."

Before Russell could decide, the bedroom door was flung open and Gloria Russell appeared on the threshold, a vision in red leather: boots, mini tube skirt, vest.

"We'll go," she said.

Tedesco gulped. He couldn't take his eyes off her.

"I don't think it's a good idea," Russell told his wife.

"We need to put this behind us. I'll be all right. Don't worry."

"Are you sure?"

They talked across Tedesco, and the look that passed between them surprised him. It indicated a much stronger bond than he'd had any inkling existed.

Danny Neel called on Rollo Dubois.

Ochs was responsible for getting Herb Cranston.

Norah, along with Arenas and Galinas and the tape, waited back in Studio A.

It was set up as it had been the night of the murder: electronic keyboard in the center and mike beside it. Although the backup singers and the band were not there, additional mikes and chairs represented them. It was hard to imagine that the magic that captivated millions of people and earned billions of dollars could be created in this big, bare room, Norah thought. It was hard to credit that the people she had summoned and who now sat uneasily on folding chairs had the talent to create it. They appeared so very ordinary. But of course, they weren't. They were led to believe that they were, in fact, extraordinary, that they could flout the rules without paying the price. They were thrust into an artificial world not of their making and fed on the idolatry of their fans. They were torn by stresses and spoiled by success.

Except for Norah and her team, the only outsider was Helene Galinas. The waitress was excited and awed to find herself in such company. Her attitude was indicative of the near reverence in which these people were held by the public. When Norah introduced her, they barely acknowledged Helene Galinas. Only Gloria Russell gave her more than a glance, and it was anything but friendly. The look Galinas returned showed she didn't consider the star's wife as among the hallowed.

"We'll start with you, Miss Galinas," Norah said. "On September twenty-third in the early morning, you met Ben Russell here in this studio. Is that right?"

"Yes."

"For what purpose?"

"To make a recording."

"And what happened?"

"He let me in through the back and we came up here. He showed me how everything worked, put the earphones on me—I mean, the *cans*. He explained that he had the *instrumental track* ready and I could use it as background. He would make the *mix* in the control room." She was proud of knowing and using the professional terms.

"Do we need all this?" Bo Russell interrupted. "We're familiar with the process. I thought you were just going to ask a couple of questions . . ."

"The questions will come, Mr. Russell. Go on, Helene. Where were you positioned?"

"Right here." She went over to one of the microphones set up for the backup singers.

"And Ben Russell was in the control room?"

"Yes."

"And then?"

"He turned a switch and the music just welled up in my ears. It possessed me. I'll never forget the feeling. For a moment I was lost. I had no idea what I was supposed to do. Then I saw Ben pointing at me, and I started to sing."

"Were you able to complete the number?"

"No. The phone rang."

"I thought you said you had the earphones—uh, the cans on. If the music was coming through, how could you hear the telephone?"

"I didn't. Ben cut off the music and waved at me to stop. I saw him pick up the phone in the control room. When he was through, he came into the studio, very excited. He said Bo had called for a session. We had to stop and I had to get out."

All eyes turned to Bo.

"Go on," Norah said.

"Well, while I was collecting my things, I heard Mrs. Russell on the front stairs."

"Mrs. Gloria Russell?"

"Sure. Who else?"

"Wait a minute. Hold it." Russell was on his feet. "What's going on here, Lieutenant?"

"Sit down, Mr. Russell." Norah addressed the waitress. "You saw Mrs. Gloria Russell on the stairs?"

"No ma'am. I heard her."

"Ah . . ." With a grunt and a shake of his head, Russell dismissed that and did sit down again.

"How can you be sure it was Mrs. Russell?" Norah asked.

"First of all, she cried out, 'It's me, Gloria.' "

Russell shrugged. "Anybody could have said she was Gloria."

"Why? Why would anyone do that?" Norah wanted to know.

"I have no idea. I'm only pointing out it's possible."

"Oh, it was her, all right," Helene broke in. "It wasn't the first time I'd heard her scream for Ben. One morning while I was clearing his breakfast trolley, she walked into his room and accused us of having sex."

"And were you?"

The girl was pink with embarrassment, but at the same time proud. "I wasn't the only one. He'd dumped her a long time ago."

Russell was on his feet again. "That's enough. Come on, Gloria, we're leaving."

His wife didn't respond. She remained transfixed in her chair.

"You'll get a chance to refute all this, Mr. Russell," Norah assured the star.

"What's to refute? My wife and my brother were going together way back before I married Gloria. That's no secret, never was. As for the rest of it, the girl's lying. She says my wife was here, but she didn't see her. She heard her voice!" His lips twisted in a derisive smile. "Even if she claimed she'd seen Gloria, it would only be her word. You can't prove anything."

"Want to bet, Mr. Russell?"

His blue-gray eyes narrowed, his round face sagged; from cherub he became fallen angel. "Stop hinting. Say what you have to say."

"I will if you'll stop interrupting." Norah made a point of waiting till he sat down once more. Then she turned her attention to Rollo Dubois. "Having lived with Duggie Watts, toured and worked with him for several months, you were certainly familiar with the routine he followed when taking part in a recording session—despite the fact that you're not yourself a sound engineer?"

"Of course."

"Good. I would like you to step outside the studio and then come in as though you were Duggie Watts and do what he usually did. In other words, I'd like you to retrace his steps."

Rollo Dubois nodded and went out into the corridor. In a matter of moments, he appeared behind the glass partition separating studio from control room. He went over to the far board and flipped a switch. "The first thing Duggie would do was put the studio lights on, but they're already on."

"All right. What else?" Norah asked. "Is anything else different?"

"Well, we're talking back and forth, so that means the main studio mike is live. I just put it on."

"And it wouldn't have been on when he first entered?"

"No. Everything would have been turned off when we left, naturally."

"But if somehow, for some reason, something had been on, left live, Mr. Watts would have noticed?"

"For sure. He checked his board first thing."

"And he could tell at a glance if anything was out of line? Like a pilot checking the control panel of his plane?"

"Exactly."

"Thank you, Mr. Dubois. You may come back and join us."

She waited for him before addressing the group.

"Your rehearsal broke at eleven p.m. the night of the twenty-second. The next call was for eleven the following morning—that would have been the twenty-third. Everyone left but Ben. He had promised Miss Galinas to help her make a demo. The studio was on lockout, so this seemed the perfect opportunity. He waited till everybody was gone, then called her and told her to come over. He figured to get the recording done and have plenty of time for other things—most of the night."

Norah paused, scanning the faces around her.

"However, at approximately three-thirty a.m., as he was working in his suite at the hotel, Bo Russell was blessed with inspiration and decided he was ready to 'lay down tracks.' He contacted Mr. Cranston and ordered him to get the group together. Naturally, Ben was the first Mr. Cranston called. He didn't find him in his room. He tried various other possible hangouts and finally located him here. His call interrupted Ben and Miss Galinas during the recording."

Bo Russell immediately turned on his manager. "Why didn't you tell me? You let me think you contacted Ben at the hotel. What was the point?"

"I didn't want to embarrass you."

"Embarrass me? Why should it embarrass me? I knew what Ben used the studio for. You think I haven't got eyes in my head?"

"I'm sorry, Bo."

"Yeah, sure. I know you are."

"Mr. Cranston," Norah continued, "you informed Ben Russell that his brother had called a rehearsal to begin at five a.m. and that the company and Bo himself would be arriving anytime. Is that right?"

"Yes ma'am."

"So in the hurry of getting rid of Miss Galinas, it's

possible he might have forgotten to turn off the studio mike and overlooked the fact that tracking tape was still running?"

"It's possible."

"Even likely," Norah commented. She addressed Rollo Dubois again. "When Bo arrived with the keys, you and Mr. Watts were the first to enter the building. You came into the studio and Mr. Watts went directly to the control room. Right?"

"Right."

"He noticed immediately that the switch position of one of the mikes was wrong and also that a tape was running. Automatically, he turned them off. He knew he hadn't left the board like that and he didn't think the house engineer had either. It wasn't hard to guess who had. He had no time to play the tape then, so he set it aside to listen to later."

She looked around. Everyone appeared to follow her reasoning and accept it. So far.

"When he finally got around to playing the tape, what Duggie Watts heard was not just a recording by an amateur singer but a recording of a murder being committed."

Delving into her handbag, Norah held up the cassette. "It's all here—Miss Galinas's rendition, the interruption—you won't hear the telephone because it rang in the control room, not the studio, but you will hear Mrs. Russell as she burst in on Miss Galinas and Ben. You will hear the quarrel between Gloria Russell and Ben Russell, and finally you will hear the shot that killed Ben Russell. All of it is on this tape. This is the basis for Duggie Watts's blackmail demand."

Gloria Russell stared at the cassette. "No. It was erased."

"Shh. Be quiet," her husband warned.

Norah's heart pounded. "Didn't it occur to you, Mrs. Russell, that Watts would have made copies?"

"Oh my God!"

"Tapes can be doctored, Gloria," Russell warned. "It's a trick."

"Would you like to hear it?" Norah challenged.

Bo saw his wife was dazed. He shrugged. "It's meaningless, but go ahead."

Norah handed the cassette to Ferdi, who went around to the control room and gave it to the house engineer. Moments later, after a short instrumental introduction, Helene Galinas's reedy voice filled the studio with a thin, psychedelic melody:

> *Take my heart,*
> *Love me.*
> *Hold me.*
> *I'm yours.*

An interlude in which trumpets whined, then the drums rolled and exploded. A couple of beats and the voice quavered:

> *I yearn for you*
> *No matter what you do,*
> *Even if you're untrue*
> *I'll love you always.*
> *Take my heart . . .*

"That's enough! Stop. Turn it off." Bo Russell signaled the engineer. He whirled on Norah. "I did it. I did it, all right? Tell him to shut the damn thing off. Kill it."

Norah nodded to Ferdi, and at his nod the engineer complied. But the sound lingered. The beat echoed relentlessly from the amplifiers. Norah winced. She had to wait till the last vestige of sound was stilled before she could speak.

"You killed your brother. Why?"

Bo swallowed a couple of times. "Because he wouldn't leave Gloria alone."

"You knew they had resumed their affair?"

"I heard rumors—I'm not deaf. A lot of people resented Ben because he had special privileges. They were jealous and tried to make trouble between us, but I didn't believe them. Then that Wednesday morning when I walked into the studio building, I heard Ben and Gloria yelling at each other. There couldn't be any doubt about the relationship. And there couldn't be any doubt that Gloria wanted to end it and he didn't. He was forcing himself on her and she was resisting."

"When did all this happen?"

"If you mean what time, I don't know. Time doesn't mean much to me when I'm working."

"It was three forty-five a.m. when you called Mr. Cranston. Did you come right over?"

"No. I jotted down a few notes, a few ideas, to make sure I didn't lose them. It could have taken thirty minutes or so. I don't think it was more than that, probably less."

"Go on."

"I crept upstairs. I needn't have bothered—they wouldn't have heard me if I'd come in with a drumroll. Gloria told Ben it was over, finished. She threatened that if he didn't leave her alone, she would tell me. Ben laughed. He laughed and told her to go ahead. 'Go ahead,' he said. 'Tell him what you want and while you're at it tell him we've been fucking each other practically since your wedding night. He isn't going to believe it.' "

Bo paused. His high color deepened into scarlet, a dangerous scarlet.

Gloria got up and went to him. She stood close and whispered, "It's not true. We didn't. Not after you and I were married." Her whole body trembled. "I swear it, Bo. I swear it."

"It's all right. I know. I know that now. But at the time . . ." He put a hand up to his eyes as though to fend off the remembrance and swayed slightly.

Cranston moved quickly to support him and return him to his chair. Ferdi ran in from the control room.

"Don't say another word," Cranston counseled. "He should have his lawyer," he protested to Norah.

But the star was deep into his catharsis. "Even so, I was ready to turn my back on both of them and walk away. Then he hit her. The studio is soundproof, naturally, but they'd left the door wide open, so I could not only hear everything but see what was going on. He knocked her to the floor. He kicked her. He kicked her in the *stomach*. He could have injured her permanently. He could have killed the *baby*."

A soft gasp from those assembled was followed by a stunned silence.

"Read Mr. Russell his rights, Sergeant," Norah said.

Ferdi did so, taking care to speak slowly and clearly, but Russell did not appear to take it in.

"Do you understand these rights as they've been explained to you?" Norah asked.

"Yes."

"He doesn't. You can see he doesn't." Again Cranston tried to shield the star.

Norah ignored him. "You fired once at your brother, is that right, Mr. Russell?"

"Yes."

"How did you happen to be carrying a gun?"

"I carry a gun regularly since I got mugged four months ago."

"Are you carrying it now?"

"No. I got rid of it."

She didn't pursue that line, but quickly returned to his earlier statement. "You shot your brother once and he went down. Is that right?" Would he stand by it? She waited anxiously.

"That's right."

A jolt passed through her. It was a staggering admission, but he didn't realize it. She held very still. The team had caught it, of course, and were equally careful not to betray their excitement.

"I didn't mean to kill him," Bo Russell pleaded. "I didn't even realize he was dead. I kept waiting for him to get up, to move, to say something, but he just lay there. I went over to him. I knelt beside him. I wanted to help him. His eyes were wide open—he looked surprised."

He probably was, Norah thought. "So then?"

"I didn't know what to do. I needed time to think. People would be walking in for the session at any moment. I had to do something."

"So you hid the body. You dragged it into the isolation booth. He was a big man, dead weight—did your wife help?"

"No! I did it myself."

"All right. You got the body into the isolation booth, then you took Mrs. Russell downstairs and let her out the back way. What about the gun? You didn't have it on you when we searched."

"I gave it to Gloria to take away. Later on . . . I took a walk across the Fifty-ninth Street bridge and dropped it over the side."

A fact that could be neither proved nor disproved, Norah thought.

"So after you put Mrs. Russell in a cab and sent her

back to the hotel, you went around to the front as though you were just arriving. Watts and Dubois were waiting to be let in. You produced your key and the three of you came upstairs to this studio."

She paused.

"You say you loved Ben and you were grateful because he took care of you when you were kids, yet you rehearsed over three hours knowing he was dead and that you killed him and that his body was right here in the room with you."

"I did what I had to do."

"Did you also have to kill Duggie Watts?"

He took a while to answer. "It was an accident. The gun was his. Would you believe it? It's true, the gun was his. I'd gotten rid of mine—I told you that. Anyway, Duggie had the tape Ben and the girl had made that night and he was blackmailing me with it. He was very nervous. I guess he thought I might try to get the tape from him without paying, so he pulled his gun. In fact, that *was* my idea. In the struggle, the gun went off. He was the one who got shot."

Chapter 16

Maybe Watts *had* been killed with his own gun, Norah thought. In this sad, crazy case it was crazy enough to be true. It was a defense that would be difficult to disprove. She should be satisfied that the confrontation had worked as planned and had drawn a confession from Bo Russell. Duggie Watts had not made copies. The one and only tape, the master, had been erased as Gloria Russell had inadvertently revealed. The tape Norah used as a decoy had been made that very evening by Helene Galinas over at Fidelity, duplicating her earlier performance. There was nothing else on it but her voice: not the quarrel between Gloria and Ben, not Bo's arrival— though that would not have been recorded because he hadn't spoken—and not the fatal shot. If the tape had been allowed to run longer, that would have been all too evident, but Bo had taken the bait and stopped it.

The rock star was led out of the studio in handcuffs. He was followed by his wife, his manager, and Rollo Dubois. The word must have gotten out that Bo was in trouble, because his people were waiting in the street and they had attracted a crowd of the curious. Norah had not arranged for backup and for a moment she was anxious. But this was a quiet crowd, and orderly. They were there to show support. They murmured encouragement as the star passed. They watched silently as he was helped into Nick Tedesco's car for the ride to the precinct. Then they formed ranks and followed on foot.

This sudden escort brought home sharply the regard in which Bo was held. Those who worked for him were intensely loyal, and though ticket sales were off, he still had fans. If the grand jury believed that Ben had abused and assaulted Gloria and threatened the life of her unborn child, sympathy would be with Bo, and they might not even indict. The personality of the accused plus the circumstances in which the crime was committed, with particular regard to provocation, were becoming increasingly relevant. Not so long ago, they would not even have been admissible.

In the García case, Luisa García had not been in imminent physical danger when she shot her brother, but the grand jury, in spite of the prosecutor's wishes, had responded with a broad interpretation of the right to protect not only oneself but one's family and had reduced the charge. Were Gloria Russell the one charged instead of Bo, she certainly could plead self-defense, and whatever a jury might think of her morals, they would have little choice but to acquit her. In every investigation there came a time to step aside and let the prosecution take over. Norah thought she had learned that lesson. She sighed: some times were harder than others.

And Norah had her own worries. Her date with the I.A. board was drawing uncomfortably close and she continued to have an uneasy sense that she had missed a salient point in her own defense. Tedesco and Neel would be tied up for the next several hours seeing Bo Russell through arraignment. Arenas and Ochs had gone back to the squad. Alone, Norah entered the park, instinctively drawn to the Bow Bridge. Looking out across the narrow neck of water, she reviewed Jocelyn Warran's testimony and traced the path of her flight. It was Jocelyn Warran who had introduced the possibility of cross fire. She had felt threatened, she'd told Norah.

Norah found a phone booth and dialed the witness's number.

"I'm sorry to disturb you," she said. "I need to go over the sequence of those shots once again."

"Sure, Lieutenant. Anytime. I told you."

"Thank you. You said you heard two shots. The first was after Koster released his grip and you got to your feet and started to run. There was a considerable gap between that and the second. In fact, you were around the bend in the path and out of sight when you heard the second shot."

"Yes, that's right."

"Could there have been one more?" Norah asked. "Think about it. Could there have been a third?"

There was a pause. Norah could visualize the witness reflecting, her large hazel eyes fixed in thought.

"No," she said at last. "I don't think so." She said it slowly, sensing it was not what Norah wanted.

"I mean between the first shot and what appears to have been the second."

"Between?"

"Right after the first shot." Norah knew she was doing more than just stimulating Jocelyn Warran's memory; she was leading the witness. Well, they weren't in the court-room, after all. "Close after. Almost simultaneously."

"Like an echo?"

"Yes. Yes. Like an echo."

"It's possible."

The painful tightness across Norah's chest eased as the air rushed out of her lungs and she could breathe again.

"Thank you, Ms. Warran. Thank you very much."

Jocelyn Warran had admitted it could have happened. That was all Norah needed.

In the squad room, Norah explained.

"The girl was running away. She was no danger to Koster. I was prepared to arrest him, so I *was*. I drew my gun, he drew his. We fired almost simultaneously. He missed. I got him in the shoulder and he went down. I crossed the bridge and ran to him and discovered he was only wounded. I told him to stay where he was, that I was going for help. Just before I reached the phone, I turned and there he was on his feet again, gun in hand and aiming at me. I fired, and that was not the second but the third shot."

She looked around. "The first and third bullets were from my gun and they have been retrieved. The second shot came from Koster's piece. The gun is gone, but maybe we can find the bullet."

There was an awkward silence.

"Excuse me, Lieutenant, I don't mean to rain on your parade, but it's a little farfetched," Sutphin said. Officially he was still carrying the case and was also summoned to give evidence before the I.A. on the next afternoon.

"But not impossible," Norah countered. "The witness, Jocelyn Warran, agrees there could have been three shots—the first two close together, the third after a considerable interval."

"You were the one who said there were two," Sutphin reminded her.

"I was agitated. I had just killed a man and then been told he was unarmed."

"He was, Lieutenant." Sutphin actually looked sorry for her.

"The body was unattended while I was on the phone to nine-one-one. Someone could have come by, seen the gun lying on the ground, and taken it. All right, it's a big coincidence, but we can't rule it out. On the other hand, it's a lot less likely that a passerby would spot a spent bullet, even less that he would pick it up and take it."

"You think it's still there," Ferdi Arenas concluded.

"It has to be."

"Assuming it exists," Sutphin muttered.

Norah looked straight at him. "Let's assume it."

Al Sutphin's eyes narrowed; his jaw clenched. Then he shrugged.

"Good," Norah said, and that ended the exchange. The round was hers, but she didn't really care about rounds or points. She addressed him now along with the others as a group.

"I know where I stood and where he stood. Assuming he fired, we know that he missed me. The bullet must have hit somewhere past me—the trunk of a tree, a bench, a lamppost."

"Or it arced and fell to the ground and buried itself in rotted leaves and mud and God knows what other detritus. Or it fell into the lake." Sutphin couldn't restrain himself. "In which case it can lie there forever."

She continued as though he hadn't spoken. "There should be enough light to search by . . . six-thirty. Let's say seven. We'll need a couple of metal detectors."

Arenas and Ochs nodded.

"So we'll meet at the Bow Bridge at seven."

Ferdi followed her to the door. "Anything I can do for you in the meantime?"

Norah hesitated. "No, nothing. Thanks, Ferdi. I'm going home to grab some sleep."

"Good idea. Give you a ride?"

"I'll walk, thanks. I need the air."

Friday, October 2
5:30 a.m.

But Norah didn't go home. Though she didn't expect anything to happen till daylight, she nevertheless returned to the park to keep watch. The hours passed slowly. It was cold. She shivered in her light jacket. She was stiff. She needed to move around and get the blood circulating, but of course, she didn't dare take the chance. She was too numb even to think. Actually, there was nothing to think about—either he took the bait or he didn't. If he did, then she was right and her problems were over. In spite of that, she almost wished he wouldn't turn up.

Taking care to shield the luminous dial of her watch, Norah pushed her sleeve back to see the time. Five-thirty. Light would be breaking soon. If anything was going to happen, that's when it would be.

She had taken a position at the foot of the gentle slope of Cherry Hill. This was where she had been when the girl, followed by Koster, emerged from the thick growth on the other side. If Koster had indeed fired at Norah and missed, where would the bullet have been most likely to hit? He had been standing on slightly lower ground. Therefore, tracing an upward trajectory, she decided it would have landed in one of a clump of pines directly behind her. It shouldn't be difficult to find. The beam of a flashlight should reveal it.

Suppose he didn't come? Norah worried. Would that be proof he was innocent? Or an indication that he was

smart enough to smell the trap? Just as she had convinced herself that he wasn't coming after all, the taste
of disappointment bitter in her mouth, she sensed movement in the area of the Bethesda Fountain. Then she
saw him. He was crossing the pavement and coming
toward her slowly, a shadow among shadows. As he approached, the sky growing lighter behind him, he
emerged from the mass and took individual form. He
was a big, shambling man. Though she couldn't make
out his features or coloring, Norah had no doubt who
it was. His gait, both knees flexed to distribute the weight
and ease the pain of supporting that heavy, hulking
body, was distinctive. He proceeded at a very slow pace,
as though he were merely enjoying the cool of the morning.

Norah hunkered down closer to the shrubbery. Despite his awkwardness and his bad legs, the strength in
his overlong arms more than compensated. He was a
powerful man. She held her breath and was relieved
when he passed without so much as glancing in her
direction. He was lost to her view for several moments.
Too long? As she strained to see, he reappeared at the
foot of the hill, where Norah herself had stood on the
night of the interrupted rape. He took the position that
would have had him looking across at the would-be rap-
ist, just as she had described it a few hours ago in the
squad room. Suddenly, she saw a narrow beam of light
moving up and down the trunk of one of the trees.

From the first, he went to the second, then stopped
and held the light steady.

He'd found it!

His back was to her, so Norah couldn't be sure what
he was doing, but she supposed he was trying to pry the
bullet out with his fingers. For heaven's sake, didn't he
have a penknife? Sure enough, he reached into the side

pocket of his windbreaker. The movement of his arm indicated he was scooping away the tree bark. Carefully, he drew the bullet out.

"What have you got there, Al?" Norah called, stepping away from the shrubbery to reveal herself.

He turned. There were no more shadows. They faced each other across an open stretch of field in the flat light of dawn.

"What have I got where?" he asked, putting his left hand behind his back.

"In your hand. In your left hand."

Stretching out his arm, he opened his hand. "You mean this?" At the same time, with his right hand he reached into his shoulder holster for his gun. "You want to tell me how you figured it out?"

Norah's eyes were fixed on the gun. "Oh, I've known for some time you took the gun off the body." Despite her determination to control it, her voice quavered. "It wasn't likely to have been some stranger who happened to pass by. Nobody believed that. I certainly didn't. When I phoned in, you caught the squeal. You were the first one on the scene. Except for Doc Jasper, you and Tedesco were the only ones who touched the body. Doc had no reason to remove the gun. Neither did Nick. But you did. You made it very clear that you had it in for me. I couldn't believe you'd go to such lengths to get even, but I guess it was too good an opportunity to miss. All you had to do was say there was no gun on the body and then walk away with it in your pocket. I knew it right away, but I didn't have proof."

"You still don't."

With a high and wide swing of his left arm, Al Sutphin hurled the small lump of metal across the path and into the water beyond. Norah watched the arc of flight and heard the plink as the slug broke the surface and sank.

"We'll find it."

"You won't be around to direct the search," Sutphin sneered. "You think you're invincible, Mulcahaney. You think nothing can touch you, nothing can hurt you. You're about to find out how wrong you are." He raised the gun.

"You won't get away with this."

"Maybe, maybe not. You'll never know."

"Do you honestly think I came out here without backup?" Norah asked.

"Sure. That's your style. You're full of yourself. You work alone—you don't share the glory."

The words stung. "I don't risk my life. Take a look behind you."

He laughed. It was a short bark, contemptuous. "You expect me to fall for that old chestnut? I'm insulted. I really am, Ms. Mulcahaney."

"Don't be." Ferdi Arenas emerged from behind an outcropping of rock on the hill above Sutphin.

Still covering Norah, Sutphin took a quick glance over his shoulder to identify the new threat. "Oh hell, it's you! The snitch," he sneered. "I might have known the two of you would gang up on me."

Ferdi's face was set; his dark eyes gleamed. "I followed the lieutenant from the station house," he said, holding on to his temper. "She didn't know I was here."

"Of course she didn't," Sutphin scoffed.

"If she'd asked for backup, I don't know anybody in the squad who would have turned her down. But she didn't ask. She didn't ask because she didn't want to put anybody in the position of trapping a buddy, a position she was forced into—in case you didn't know."

"How sweet."

"Yes, that's what it is, but I don't expect you to understand. Drop the gun, Al, the game's over." Ferdi tapped his chest, indicating the location of the recorder. "It's all here—how you tried to frame the lieut' by with-holding evidence. The only thing missing is motive. Why did you do it? You want to tell us, or should I guess?"

"Guess all you want."

"It couldn't be because she ID'd you on the video. Captain Jacoby had done that ahead of her. You didn't go after him."

Sutphin shrugged.

"Because she's a woman," Ferdi suggested.

"Hell, no. Don't try to pin that sex discrimination shit on me."

"Why then?" Norah asked. "What did I ever do to you?"

Suddenly, Sutphin spun around and spit in her face. "You turned me into a cripple."

"What?"

"You kept me on desk duty. You never assigned me to any of the big cases."

"I tried to spare you because of your health."

"Who asked you?"

"I thought . . . your knees . . ."

"My knees are all right. I can walk as good as anybody. I can run. You advised against my promotion. You ru-ined my career. My wife left me."

"Your knees were okay after the operation, yes. Are they now? You've stopped working out. You're out of shape. You're drinking. If I put you on the street, you'd be a risk to the men and women working with you."

"That's a lie." Nevertheless, he was shaken.

"It's the truth and you know it."

They formed a triangle on the hillside. Ferdi had not drawn his gun; in fact, he stood with hands open and turned outward to show he was unarmed. How far did she dare to go before Sutphin started shooting out of sheer frustration?

"The bullet you just now dug out of the tree didn't come from Koster's gun," she told Sutphin. "I came here last night and fired it into the tree for you to find. All you needed to do was turn it over to me. I couldn't show it came from Koster's gun, and you would have been in the clear."

"Drop it, Al," Ferdi said. "If you shoot one of us, the other is sure to get you."

Chapter 17

Friday, October 2
4:00 p.m.

The celebration of the dismissal of charges against Lieutenant Norah Mulcahaney began as the day shift ended; it was held at Vittorio's, a longtime precinct hangout. Chief Felix put in an appearance, but contrary to his custom, he didn't stay long. He drew Norah off to a corner, and after a brief and what appeared to be serious discussion, Jim Felix left.

Manny Jacoby, on the other hand, stayed longer than he usually did at such affairs. He seemed to be making an effort to take part and even to enjoy himself. He also watched Norah. After Chief Felix left, she remained alone. Jacoby slid off his barstool and, carrying a glass of beer—also unusual, for he seldom drank—went over to her.

"You look worried. What's the matter?"

"Al Sutphin blamed me for all his troubles," she said. "It was my fault he didn't get the big assignments. The more I tried to shield him so that he wouldn't get in over his head, the more he felt patronized. He started to drink, and he blamed me for that. It was my fault his wife walked out on him. In his eyes I was responsible for it all. But the other men, the ones who made the phone calls, who threatened me, who wrote those terrible letters, who even tried to spoil my chances to adopt . . . What did I ever do to them?"

"Nothing," Jacoby replied. "They identified with Sutphin and took their resentments out on you the same as he did. Forget about them. Think about your friends." He gestured, taking in the room at large. "All these people here tonight are trying to make up to you for what the other guys did. You should show your appreciation by having a good time. You owe it to them. With that purpose in mind"—Manny Jacoby got up and made a stiff bow—"may I have this dance?"

"Captain, I'm honored."

She had never seen him dance, didn't know that he could. Norah herself wasn't much of a dancer. Nevertheless, they began—awkwardly, keeping to the edge of the space that had been cleared for dancing, concentrating on not stepping on each other's feet. Somehow, before they were aware of it, the other couples had pulled back and they were alone in the center of the floor. Mercifully, the record ended. Amidst applause and a few good-natured cheers, Jacoby accompanied Norah back to her seat, but it wasn't long before she was out on the floor again with Julius Ochs. One after another, she danced with every man on the squad. What had started as a quiet show of support turned into an enthusiastic celebration. Yet no matter how hard she tried, Norah's heart wasn't in it.

At last it was Ferdi's turn. "You're not enjoying yourself," he observed.

"It's been a long day." She stopped. "If you don't mind, I'll just slip away."

"I'll take you home," he offered. "I have to leave myself. I told Concepción I'd be home by five, and here it is nearly seven."

"In that case, thanks."

They were silent during the short drive. When Ferdi pulled up in front of Norah's building, neither one made a move to get out. Ferdi turned in his seat.

"Want to talk?"

She sighed heavily. "I've made a mistake, Ferdi, a big mistake. I was distracted by my own personal problems and I missed the signals."

He knew she was talking about the Rocker case. "You made a logical reconstruction and Russell confessed. What more do you want?"

"The truth."

"How are you going to get it?"

"I don't know."

"Are you even absolutely sure you don't already have it?"

"No."

"Then let it go."

"I can't."

"What exactly is it that bothers you?"

"For one thing, Bo was too eager to confess. The tape was only into the second chorus when he jumped in and said to stop it. But he had nothing to fear from letting it run. His voice wasn't on it."

Ferdi frowned. "You mean it wasn't on the original? The master?"

"That's right. Bo was outside in the corridor while his wife and Ben were inside the studio. The door was open. He watched and listened, but he didn't speak."

"Would he just stand there and shoot his brother who had watched over and protected him when they were orphans, and whom he loved and indulged, without so much as a word about why he was doing it?"

"In the stress of what was happening—yes. But for the sake of argument, let's say he called out to Ben to stop hitting Gloria. He was out of range of the mike.

What bothers me most is that he admits to only one shot. We know that there were two."

They were both silent for a while.

"Then there's Watts's blackmail attempt," Norah went on.

"What about it?"

"How do you explain it? If Bo's voice wasn't on the tape, then Watts had no hold on him."

Ferdi scowled. "Was he blackmailing Gloria?"

"We have to ask ourselves: Why did Gloria go to the studio that night? She never attended rehearsals. Why did she go on that particular occasion?"

"Because she knew Ben had a date with his latest girl-friend and she was jealous."

"No."

"No? I give up," Ferdi said. "I give up and so should you. At least for tonight."

It was still early, but Norah went right to bed. She was bone weary, aching, too tired even to make herself a sandwich or heat up some soup. For the first time in over a week she wasn't under threat of disciplinary action by I.A.: she had been completely vindicated. Everyone was satisfied with her solution of the Rocker case. Chief Deland had singled her out for commendation. Once again, she was the media's darling.

But she couldn't sleep.

What kept Norah awake was a thing so small, so sub-jective, a mental burr, that she hadn't even mentioned it to Ferdi, but the more she dwelt on it, the more it irritated. It was Bo Russell's reply when she'd asked him how he happened to have a gun on him the night of the murder of his brother. He said he carried it regularly since being mugged and he had a license for it. He made a point of that. He was confessing to murder and also making sure they knew he had a legal right to carry the murder weapon. To Norah, it was the reaction of an innocent man.

She threw back the covers, swung her legs over the side of the bed, and sat up. By putting his wife's jewelry up for collateral, Bo Russell had made the million-dollar bail. He'd also provided the court with his schedule of concert dates. His lawyer had argued that Russell would not risk the damage to his career by failing to fulfill the commitments. Nor would he risk the success of a credible and sympathetic defense by not showing up for trial, Norah thought. Tomorrow Bo Russell and The Earth Shakers would start a cross-country trek which would end in San Diego. Tonight they were in Queens, still within easy reach.

Friday, October 2
10:00 p.m.

It was a big stadium and Bo Russell had had little expectation of filling it, but the notoriety of the charge against him attracted others besides his usual fans. For the first time in nearly a year, Bo Russell and The Earth Shakers were playing to capacity. In the not-so-distant past, Norah thought, the Victorians had delighted in shuddering with the vicarious thrill of viewing waxen likenesses of murderers in dark, macabre settings appropriate to their crimes. Our present-day killers were put on stage in person and the spotlights turned on them. They were interviewed on television. They were paid huge sums for rights to their life stories which were turned into docu-dramas and broadcast coast to coast for the nation's entertainment.

When Norah arrived at the outermost parking field, the show was in full swing. The sound, electronically amplified, shattered the night. She winced, wished for earplugs, and marveled at how the neighbors could tolerate it. The laser beams were flashes of colored lightning, dazzling and blinding even at that distance. Her ID got Norah past the roadblocks to the V.I.P. parking. The only space available was in the reserved section. She pulled up, got out of the car, and started to lock up.

"Hey! You can't park there," a young man with long hair and horn-rimmed glasses called out. He was standing just outside what Norah took to be the stage entrance.

She walked over to him, open shield case in hand. "Who are you?"

"Assistant stage manager." His clipboard was his badge.

"What time does the show break?" she asked.

"Depends."

"On what?"

"Depends on the crowd. How they react. How willing Bo is to do encores. They feed off one another—the artist and the audience."

He paused and they both listened. The star was well into the gospel music segment of his program. It was Bo's favorite and the style with which he was identified. Passion and intensity throbbed in his voice. He was working the crowd out of their seats, turning the vast arena into a tent-show revival meeting. Suddenly he stopped. The lights went out. The crowd was smothered by the silence. Then, one by one, from different sections of the stand, screams, cheers, and applause broke out and swelled into one pulsing paean of adulation.

"It could be a long night," the stage manager said with awe.

"Where is Mr. Russell's dressing room?"

"You can't . . ."

Norah just looked at him.

He shrugged and stood aside, pointing down a long, narrow corridor. "Last door on the right. But he won't see you. He won't see anybody before or after a show."

Norah was already walking away.

Through the glass panel in the dressing room door, she could see the bluish flicker that indicated the television was on. It showed Bo at the microphone, legs planted firmly and slightly apart, arms flung out, head back—offering himself to his worshipers. It was a closed-circuit transmission of what was happening on stage.

Norah knocked. And knocked again. She tried the doorknob. It turned and she went in. It was the usual plain, bare room with a big, well-lit dressing table on one wall, a washbasin and a rack of Bo Russell's glittering costumes on the other. Gloria Russell sat in the far corner. Norah had expected her to be sitting out in the audience basking in her husband's reflected glory. But it was immediately evident she was in no condition for it. Her head was slumped forward, chin resting on her chest. Beside her on a small trunk that served as a table was a nearly empty highball glass.

"Mrs. Russell?" Norah went over and touched her shoulder gently. "Are you all right?"

Gloria Russell opened her eyes. They were unfocused. The black mascara had run and left dark streaks on her thick white foundation. She looked at Norah without recognition. After a few moments, the mists cleared. She shook herself, sat a little straighter, and reached for the glass. She swallowed and made a face.

"Slop." Leaning heavily on the armrests, she got herself to her feet and over to a small, portable liquor case. "What would you like, Lieutenant?"

"Nothing, thanks."

"That's not a good sign, is it?" Her speech was slurred. "That means you're on duty, right?"

"It means I don't want a drink."

"Oops! Excuse me." She carried the bottle to where she'd been sitting and placed it on the trunk. "So, what *do* you want?"

"I want to know why you went to the recording studio on the night of your brother-in-law's murder."

"What?"

"I want to know—"

"I heard what you said. I don't understand the question. Bo had called a rehearsal." Pouring fresh liquor over the dregs in the glass, she dismissed the matter.

"It was not your practice to attend rehearsals, particularly at such an hour. You told me yourself you weren't about to get out of bed every time Bo had a burst of inspiration."

"This time I did."

"Why? How did you even find out about it? As far as you knew, the next call was for eleven in the morning. What brought you to the studio before dawn? Herb Cranston didn't notify you—not then, not ever. Why should he? You're not part of the group. Why did you go to the studio?"

Gloria Russell remained silent.

"You went to see Ben. You knew he'd be there with his latest. You were jealous. You went to confront him."

"Don't be ridiculous."

She didn't really seem to care, Norah thought as she continued to test the rock star's wife.

"You married Bo because you couldn't get his brother. For a while, you were happy. You basked in Bo's fame. It was exciting to travel and share in his success. But it paled. Bo was working hard—he didn't have much time for you. You began to feel left out. You watched Ben playing around with other women. He flaunted them in front of you. Somehow, almost inevitably, the two of you started up again. And then you got pregnant. As usual, Ben refused responsibility. He advised you to tell Bo the child was his.

"And Bo was ecstatic. He couldn't do enough for you. He treated you like a queen, so that finally you realized where your interests lay. You decided to break it off with Ben once and for all.

"But it wasn't so easy. Ben needed money. He always needed money—for women, for gambling. This time he owed some dangerous people. He tried to get the money by skimming the box office receipts, but Herb Cranston was watching too closely. He couldn't go to Bo—Bo was having his own financial problems. When Bo paid off Daisy Barth, he'd warned Ben that the well was dry. So? Ben turned to you. You had jewelry you could pawn or sell. If you didn't get the money for him, he threatened to tell Bo who the baby's real father was."

Norah paused to gauge Gloria Russell's reaction. Was the alcohol padding the shock? In the brief hiatus, one of the pieces that had seemed irrelevant earlier assumed significance and fell neatly into place.

"Bo stated that after being mugged four months ago he applied for and was granted a license to carry a gun. He insisted that he carried it at all times. My guess is, he hardly ever carried it. The gun made him nervous. He put it in a bureau drawer and left it there. He didn't even lock the drawer.

"Did you stop to think of the trouble you would make for Bo by using his gun? Did you care?"

The witness was sobering, and with sobriety came a look of caution in her eyes.

Norah continued, "You went to the studio with the

intention of making one last effort to reason with Ben. You waited till he got rid of this girlfriend. Then you explained that you couldn't get the kind of money he needed. You couldn't sell or pawn your jewelry without Bo finding out sooner or later. Anyway, you weren't disposed to sell. You begged him to at least give you a little time. He wouldn't listen. So you took the gun out of your purse and pointed it at him. He didn't believe you'd use it. He had you in thrall—for years you'd been at his beck and call. He owned you, or so he thought. Even at that moment, he tried to seduce you. Isn't that so?"

The high color of humiliation rose and suffused the heavy white makeup. "I told him no. I told him it was over. He threw me to the floor and came down on me. I fought him off. He kicked me. That's when Bo burst in and shot him."

Even now, knowing what she knew, it sounded reasonable, Norah thought. "No. You shot Ben. It was you. He was going to rape you, wasn't he? And you shot him."

Gloria Russell raised her dark, smoldering eyes to Norah. "If I shot him, how did I manage to drag him to the isolation booth and stuff him inside? He was a big man. I didn't have the strength."

"You got help. You called Bo."

She gaped, then made a sound that might have been a laugh but was closer to a bark. "Never. Never in this world would I have done such a thing. Why? Why would I? Tell me that. Why didn't I just leave him where he was and walk out?" She picked up her glass and drank deeply.

The two women faced each other in the cramped quarters of the dressing room. Outside there was the crashing thunder of applause. Sixty-six thousand voices roared. Neither one of them heard.

Norah sidestepped the challenge. "It was you Duggie

Watts was blackmailing, not Bo. Bo's voice wasn't on the tape, yours was. Bo had done a lot for Duggie Watts. Watts was grateful and, like everybody else, he respected Bo. He wasn't likely to turn around and blackmail him. But he had no compunction about putting the squeeze on you.

"You made a date with Watts and went to his room, ostensibly to pay him off. Of course, first you had to hear what you were buying. Watts played the tape for you and then you shot him. You erased the tape, got rid of the gun, and let Bo take the blame for that killing, too."

No response.

Too little and too late, Norah thought, but tried again.

"One murder or two, what difference did it make?"

No reaction to that either.

"He's putting his life on the line for you. Doesn't that mean anything? Don't you care?"

Though she continued to sip the scotch, Gloria Russell was finally, desparingly, sober. "He's not doing it for me. He's doing it for the mother of his child."

Norah searched her face. "Is the baby his?"

The answer was a long time coming. Gloria looked to Norah as one woman to another—appealing for sympathy, needing another woman's understanding. "I don't know."

Norah could only sigh, and the moment passed.

"Bo won't retract his confession, no matter what. Don't even think about it." Gloria Russell's voice was hard, almost taunting. "The lawyers say there's no way he'll be convicted. They say no jury is going to convict a man who killed in defense of his pregnant wife and unborn child. So there's nothing you can do, is there?"

It was Norah's turn to consider, and she took her time. "Tell the truth," she urged. "The same defense will serve you. You'll get the same sympathy from the public and media as Bo is getting. Everybody will be on your side. Everybody will be rooting for you."

Slowly Gloria shook her head. "He'd have to know about the baby, wouldn't he?"

Norah was more saddened than shocked. "I'd say he knows already."

In the silence between them, Norah became aware of a greater silence outside.

The show was over.

Norah had appealed to Gloria Russell's sense of justice and lost. She had stressed Bo's love and the extent of the sacrifice he was prepared to make for Gloria, giving her the benefit of every doubt. Selfless love was beyond Gloria's understanding. However, as Norah read her character, the star's wife would not be content to leave well enough alone. Norah had planted the seed and there was nothing more she could do. She watched and waited.

Then, a scant twenty-four hours before Bo Russell was required by the conditions of his bail to return to the jurisdiction, there was a new and startling development.

ROCK STAR'S WIFE CONFESSES
I KILLED TO PROTECT MY BABY
GLORIA BEGS BO'S FORGIVENESS

Accompanied by husband and lawyer, Gloria Russell had turned herself in to the New York district attorney. Her picture with Bo beside her, arm protectively around her, was on every front page of the tabloids across the nation. She appeared, first with him and then alone, on every television talk show, beginning in the early morning and continuing into the night. She was interviewed by Barbara Walters.

At last she was a celebrity in her own right.

The price would come high.

Of course, she expected to get away with it. Bo had confessed in order to protect her and the baby. He stated that he'd arrived early at the studio and just happened to walk in on his wife and his brother in the midst of their quarrel. Norah believed he had come early in response to Gloria's hysterical appeal. But she'd denied it and challenged Norah to explain why she would have done such a thing. The answer had been staring Norah in the face for a long time, but she'd held back, gambling that the uncertainty would gnaw at Gloria and break her.

Gloria had called Bo for help because Ben was still alive. She had shot him in the heat of passion, but she hadn't killed him. In the cold grip of reality, she didn't have the courage to finish him off.

Bo did. And that made two shots.

Both were guilty.

Each would continue to protect the other, and the prosecution wouldn't be able to pin it on either one. They would both walk. Unless it could be shown that that had been the plan from the beginning.

In the midst of the inevitable letdown, Norah got the message she'd been both waiting for and dreading.

"This is Sister Beatrice at the Foundling Hospital, Lieutenant. I'd appreciate it if you'd give me a call as soon as you can."

That was all, but it made Norah turn cold. Since she'd made formal application to adopt Maryanne, Norah hadn't heard a word. She had been tempted to call and ask about the status of the application, but being under a cloud, she'd been afraid to precipitate an unfavorable response. Then, cleared of guilt in the Central Park shooting, praised for her handling of the Rocker case, as much lauded as she had been criticized, Norah expected good news. She watched the mail and waited for the phone to ring. And now, finally, this. She pressed the replay button on the answering machine and listened to Sister Beatrice again. The message was noncommittal, formal, impossible to interpret. Surely if it was good news, Sister Beatrice would have indicated it. Norah checked the time. Too late to call back now. It would have to wait till morning.

She didn't sleep well. She kept thinking about the child, recalled how she'd looked at Norah with those large, limpid, trusting eyes, how she'd snuggled into Norah's arms as though she belonged there, how she'd been so reluctant to let go. *Oh, dear God, please let it be all right. Please, let me have her.*

The next morning, promptly at eight, she made the call.

"Good morning, Lieutenant." Sister Beatrice sounded friendly and cheerful. "How are you?"

"Anxious," Norah answered quickly.

"Of course you are. We need to talk."

Norah's heart sank. Bad news. It could be nothing but bad.

"When can you come over?"

"Whenever you want, Sister. Right now." Get it done, she thought.

"Well, let's say nine o'clock."

"Yes, Sister, I'll be there."

She was too nervous to eat breakfast and made do with a cup of coffee. She took a long time choosing what to wear, then decided it didn't matter. How did you dress for rejection? she thought, and ended up with her best outfit—a quiet, navy suit, skirted, with a plain, white sweater. At the last moment she added the blue sapphire earrings Joe had given her on their first anniversary; for luck. She arrived downtown at the hospital twenty minutes early. Walking around the block used up only five. She might as well wait inside, she thought. She had barely given her name and seated herself when the security guard looked in her direction.

"You may go in, Lieutenant."

Suddenly she didn't want to go in. As long as she didn't know, she could go on hoping. She wanted to put the moment off.

"Lieutenant? Do you know the way?"

"Yes, thank you." She got up, turned right to an inner corridor, up one flight, and tapped at the first door.

Judging by the stack of papers in front of her, Sister Beatrice was already well into the day's work. She looked up and indicated the coffee urn on a side table. "Help yourself, Lieutenant."

Norah shook her head. She couldn't take any more suspense. "They turned me down, didn't they? They rejected my application."

The nun's rosy face beamed. "With your background and reputation? Certainly not. On the contrary, you were unanimously approved and with very little discussion."

Relief flooded over Norah, joy, and then . . ."What's the problem, Sister?"

"Maryanne is no longer available."

Norah blanched. Her heart thudded. "You said you wouldn't offer her to anybody else, not till the board ruled on my application. You assured me—"

"Calm down, Norah. We didn't offer her to anybody else. No one so much as looked at her. It was her mother. Her natural mother changed her mind about giving her up for adoption. She decided she wants to keep Mary-anne."

Again, Norah thought. Again.

"I'm sorry, but it is her right."

"I know."

"She's gotten herself a job, a place to live, and she is prepared to make a home for Maryanne. Her parents, the mother's parents, are prepared to help if needed."

"I understand." Norah got up. "Thank you for your help, Sister." She started for the door. She had to get out of there, fast.

"Sit down, Norah," Sister Beatrice called out. "Sit down, please." She waited till Norah had done so. "There is another child."

Tears sprang into Norah's eyes. Then she shook her head. "No. I can't go through this another time."

"You don't have to. You've already been approved."

The tears spilled over and ran down Norah's cheeks.